Sashmo the Great

By: Archie Martin & S. P. Smith

Dedicated to:

Brianna & Lily, wife and daughter, for helping me strive to always continue to become better and keeping God first place.

-A.M.

Shea, my wife, Wonder Woman, and Favorite thing. Papa Smurf and Frankie Sue, the angels on my shoulders.

-S.P.S.

Our Greensboro Family that have had to hear about this story for the last 11 years yet continued to encourage us.

-A.M. & S.P.S.

Special Thanks to:

Kenny Nolasco of Imajen Studios for providing our cover art.

Prologue: Enter the Beast

The sun settled behind the horizon in the far distance; however, the light did not dim. The skies remained enraged by a fierce fire that encompassed the forests of the land. The night appeared to be less dusk and more akin to an early dawn. A group of knights came marching over the hillside, keeping paces with one another. They marched in a uniform and orderly fashion. Their commander rode a horse along beside them, barking out orders. Behind the knights, tightly in tow, a large wooden cart matched their speed. On top of this cart sat a young Hydra. The Hydra's snake-like scales were entangled in a web of ropes. An aberration of the dragon species, Hydras have massive wings and a long vicious tail like a normal dragon. However, its torso gives way to five long necks housing a remarkable five separate heads. Each head houses its own brain and personality that create a far superior and smarter creature than a typical dragon.

Its five heads were each tied down independently. The Hydra squirmed and struggled to find its elusive freedom, but the binds were too tight. The knights continued to wheel the Hydra along a path leading up to a castle not far into the distance. There, the knights are greeted by their leader, the majestic King Arthur. Arthur, the King of legend who pulled the sword from the stone, the immensely powerful Excalibur. Since that time, he had reigned supremely over Camelot.

"This is the creature sire," said the knight on horseback.

As the King examined the beast, he felt the sensation of fear overtake his body for the first time since the moment he first touched Excalibur. "And how many heads does it have there? Is it truly five?"

"Five indeed sire!"

"This is the beast that Merlin has foretold of," Arthur said. "The great Wizard has seen the future of man burning in flames at the hands of a five headed dragon. The truce will not be enough to prevent the visions of the Wizard."

"What shall we do with it?"

The King paused. The weight of the moment was not lost on him. To command this order was to break a truce that had existed for generations before him. He feared what his decision may mean for his people, but he feared the beast more.

"I shall use Excalibur to cut off each head. Take them by horseback to the farthest corners of the land. Do it swiftly and go unseen. We do not want these actions to be known."

"As you wish sire."

The knights gathered in position around the terrified Hydra. It struggled and tore at the ropes that restrained it to no avail. The King's words were perfectly understood by the young Hydra's ears, and it knew that its moments were fleeting. They Hydra continued to hiss and shoot fire puffs into the air. As the knights encircled the petrified beast, the King stepped forth. He reached to his side, as he had many times in battle before, and grabbed the handle of his sword. At that very moment, if by faith, providence, destiny, or all combined, a gigantic roar tore through the fire lit sky. The knights turned, looking dreadfully at the tree line and source of the ferocious sound. There stood a giant, gorilla-like beast. Nearly nine feet tall, it towered over the men. Hair covered its large, muscular body from head to toe. It beat its chest passionately through the duration of its call. Upon completion, it moved slowly towards the knights.

"Release the Hydra!" Its voice was powerful, yet elegant at the same time. The beast continued to walk towards the knights.

"Sagamo the Sasquatch, what an unexpected visit," said the King.

"Arthur, you know I cannot allow you to do this. Your actions tonight will violate the peace that has always existed between mankind and creatures."

"With every breath this monster takes the truce is threatened," said the King. "If he is allowed to live, you are sentencing all of man to death."

"You know the Council will never allow this creature to become a threat to you Arthur. The friendship between creature and man will continue."

"You're an honorable creature Sagamo," the King clutched Excalibur tightly in his right hand. For a brief moment, he felt a source of conflict between his soul and the sword; as if the sword was speaking to him the same way it did the day he pulled it from the Rock of Caliburn. Though he respected Sagamo, he knew what he had to do. "I cannot grant your request."

"The hard way it is," Sagamo said with a hint of defeat.

The knights surrounding Arthur rushed in to engage Sagamo. As the fight ensued, it was clear the knights were outmatched by the Sasquatch. Sagamo slung them around like a child throwing toys. The knights, though out matched, were not afraid. After each blow dealt by the monstrous beast, they continued to re-engage. Sagamo managed to fight them off for some time before he was wounded. The battle raged on as Sagamo fought with the clear purpose to only defend himself. He wished not to kill the knights or Arthur. After a long and arduous fight, the knights, though bravely fought, were weakened, tired, and defeated.

Sagamo proceeded to walk over to the cart where the young Hydra still lay. The demeanor of the Hydra had calmed as its protector came forth and began to untie the seethes that had restricted it. As Sagamo untied the last rope, King Arthur rose behind him, struggling to walk as he carried himself over to the cart, but he was too late. Sagamo had finished the last knot and the Hydra wiggled itself free, let out a scream, and flew away. Its massive body disappeared into the red sky. Unbeknownst to Sagamo, Arthur had raised his sword and he was perched to attack.

"You fool," screamed Arthur as Excalibur pierced the side of the Sasquatch. Sagamo fell to his knees and then over to his side. Arthur, using Excalibur as a crutch, pulled himself to his feet. The man now towered over the beast. Arthur again clutched his sword tightly in his hand. There was a different feeling this time. This one

6

did not sense of righteousness that it had earlier. There instead was a sense of despair, shame, and failure as he raised the sword above his head once more.

"The...the truce..." whispered Sagamo, struggling to catch his breath.

"Is over my friend," Arthur said with regret as he plunged the sword downward for a final blow on the Sasquatch. He stood over Sagamo's body. "I am sorry it had to end like this," Arthur said. "But I will always put the interest of man first."

Chapter One: Greatness Slumbers

All was usual for a cold fall evening around Loch Ness as the wind whisked through the trees. People were on boats, tourists walked around with their cameras and on the far north side of the lake inside his cave, Sashmo the Sasquatch was asleep. Sashmo, grandson of Sagamo, stood just over eight feet tall. He was covered in a dirty brown fur and resembles a muscular, upright ape.

Inside his dark and damp cave, Sashmo was curled up on a pile of dead leaves and twigs. There was a small table beside him, built from scraps of wood on which a small cockatrice sat. A cockatrice is a small, two-legged serpent with the head of a rooster. It stared at the sun setting behind the tree line.

"Ki-Ki-Ki!" it shouts loudly as it was time for Sashmo the get up.

Sashmo never opened his eyes. He reached around and swatted the cockatrice off the table. Nine minutes passed and the cockatrice was once again perched on the table.

"Ki-Ki-Ki!" the cockatrice cried again. This time Sashmo rolled over. He placed his hand under the lip of the table's ledge and flipped the entire thing over. The cockatrice was flown across the cave with its feathers covering the floor along with the shattered table. Sashmo began to snore again loudly.

Just as Sashmo was getting comfortable, a stream of water shot in and soaked him. Sashmo jumped out of his homemade bed and incoherently tried to figure out what was happening.

"Sashy! Quit hitting the snooze! The sun is already setting. Scotty will be here any second to pick you up! And I'm pretty sure I see Hugin about to land."

The naturally sarcastic voice coming from outside the cave was that of Ellie the Loch Ness Monster. Ellie, short for his family name of Elliot, is a male sea serpent that resides in Loch Ness. His body was covered in opaque green scales. His neck stretched over ten feet. His four large webbed feet were connected to the rest of his body that was surprisingly small. Ellie and Sashmo had been best friends from the moment they met.

About that time, a raven swooped down and landed in front of Sashmo's cave. This raven was known as Hugin. He and his brother Munin once served as the personal spies of the great Odin. The two were now the messengers to the mythical creatures. Their job was to spread information throughout the mythical creature world. Hugin had a rolled up piece of papyrus in his mouth that he dropped right at the opening of the cave.

"Letter for Sashmo! Letter for Sashmo," said Hugin in a voice more fitting for a parrot than a raven.

"I was right! You are Hugin. So hard to tell you and Munin apart from one another. You guys should wear different colored anklets or something," said Ellie.

9

"That is all. That is all," responded Hugin.

Hugin flew away just as quickly as he had arrived. Ellie picked up the letter and entered the cave, grabbing a scepter he had acquired from a Gnome King on his way in. Sashmo was still dripping wet.

"I've got the letter from Hugin," responded Ellie.

"Oh, it *was* Hugin?"

"Yeah. I definitely prefer Munin. A lot more personality. Maybe as a new Council Member, you can make it so Munin delivers our letters?" Ellie began speaking in an over-scholarly accent, "I, Sashmo the Sasquatch, do declare that henceforth all parcels shall hereby be delivered to myself by none other than Munin."

"No one speaks like that at Council," Sashmo said. "And why are you holding a scepter?"

"That's a story for another time. But every Council member needs a scepter, right?"

"Don't you mean a King?"

"Let's not argue semantics."

Sashmo took the letter from Ellie, opened it up. It read: *"Sashmo the Sasquatch, you are summoned to the annual Mythical Creatures Convention to be held at the Fountain of Youth. Opening Remarks begin promptly at 8 pm."* Sashmo rubbed his eyes and went to lie back on his bed, not caring that it was still soaked like himself.

"How about," as Sashmo began to yawn, "you go for me? Tell them you're a Sasquatch and you have nothing to report."

"How about *you* Sasquatch-up and get ready? We've been over this. Not only is this your bloodline we're talking here, but you're representing all mythical creatures."

The Council of Mythical Creatures had been around since the days before the truce with man. The governing body of Mythical Creatures, the Council served to keep order amongst the chaos of the Mythical Creature Kingdom. In the days of Sashmo's grandfather, Sagamo, the Council had approved the great truce with mankind. After Sagamo's death at the hands of King Arthur, the Council saw somewhat of a revolution. Inheriting his place on the Council, Sashmo's father Sakemo began a close kinship with the Hydra who had escaped death thanks to Sagamo. The Hydra owed a life debt that he in turned placed with Sakemo. As Sakemo rose to Council Member, he and the Hydra implemented a new philosophy for the Mythical Creature world. No longer in a truce with man, the Council began the belief of "Never Seen, Never Bother." After centuries under the new code, man had forgotten about the mythical creatures, believing them to be exactly that, myths. In order to remain hidden from man, mythical creatures were to never meddle in the business of man. Furthermore, they must travel in the darkness unless the species could be spotted without causing a stir, such as Hugin and Munin.

After the recent passing of Sakemo, it was time for Sashmo to take his rightful spot on the Council. Sashmo would now have a voice and a vote. When the Hydra allowed it that is. On more trivial matters the representatives were allowed a vote by simple majority. On more

11

pressing issues, especially on matters dealing with the code, the Hydra got the final say.

"All that responsibility isn't for us Ellie. Who am I to decide the districts of sea serpents? Or whether North Pole Elves can mingle with South Pole Elves?"

Ellie thought for a moment and was about to agree with Sashmo when he came to his senses, "You're right. It's not for *us*. It's for you. You get this honor."

"I'm not sure what they're thinking." said Sashmo. Ellie became fed up with Sashmo's rebuttals and decided to bring out the big guns. "Fine. What kind of beast would Abby want? Let's use a visual aid. J.D., grab my easel!"

Sashmo had known Abby for almost his entire life. Ever since Sashmo was a child, his father had groomed him for the day he would inherit his position on the Council. Sashmo had accompanied his father to most of the meetings during his early years. It was at those meetings that Sashmo would come to meet Abby. Abby's father used to be a Council Member representing the Yeti. She would accompany him to meetings as well. Her long, flowing, snow white fur had stopped him in his tracks from day one. But Sashmo was a goof and had never been able to make Abby see him as more than that. They had spent all those formative years becoming great friends, but nothing more. After Sashmo had disappointed his father and they became estranged, Sashmo and Abby had only seen each other a few times.

He knew this was his time to finally see her again, but he also knew how disappointed she was in him, much like his father had been.

Out the back of the cave ran J.D., a large creature walking on all four legs. His body was the size of a small horse. He had giant, dragon-like wings, the skull of a boar with horns protruding out of either side and a tail fit for a lion. Despite the horrible miscreation of an animal, his tail was wagging, tongue hanging out of his mouth and a dog-like smile shone across his face that made his under bite extremely visible. J.D. scampered towards the back of cave and retrieved an easel in his mouth and handed it to Ellie. Ellie grabbed the easel with a disgusted look on his face as he wiped J.D.'s slobber off of one of the legs. He then grabbed a piece of paper laying nearby, placing it on the easel.

"Good Zeus, that face is one not even a mother can love," exclaimed Ellie.

Ellie grabbed a rock from the dingy cave floor and began to scribble on the paper. After a minute, Ellie flipped around the easel and it revealed a stick-figure version of Sashmo lying sloppily in his cave.

"This is you Sashy, in your natural state. Notice how unimpressive you are."

"Thanks."

"So this version of you equals this."

Ellie went back to the drawing board. Sashmo rolled his eyes as he knew what was coming next. Ellie continued to draw on the easel, eventually revealing his new work for his friend. Ellie had drawn a picture of a Yeti. The Yeti was similar in appearance to Sashmo except for her bright, white fur that is noticeably longer than that of a Sasquatch. The Yeti depicted was bent over, hysterically laughing as evident by the giant "HA HAs" drawn all around.

"Notice how hard Abby is laughing here. See the "HA HAs" everywhere," Ellie said with a sense of pride in his work. "This version of Abby barely remembers your name and definitely doesn't believe you have any business on the Council. In fact, she thinks it's comical."

"At what point does this make me feel better?" Sashmo said sarcastically.

"I'm ignoring you for time purposes. Let's look at exhibit B."

Ellie again erased the board and began to furiously work on a new creation. Ellie's masterpiece this time presented a new version of Sashmo. He looked big, bold, and muscular. He was a powerful creature that should be feared and respected. It looked nothing like Sashmo. Around him Ellie had written the words "dignity," "honor," and "respect."

"Notice here you look nothing like your natural state. This version of you is what?"

"Dignified?"

"Yes! And?"

"Honorable and respected."

"Excellent, you're keeping up nicely. It's a happy little Sashmo on his way to Council. Guess what this version of you gets?"

Ellie once again went to work. He erased his art and drew a new picture. Here he drew another version of Abby. She appeared doe-eyed and in love as evident by her oversized heart-shaped eyes.

"Boom! What do you see?"

"A 1950's Disney princess version of Abby?"

"Exactly! And you my friend, the beast."

"Point made. I'll get ready." Sashmo headed back into his cave.

Ellie turned and looked back at his artwork yet again. His head tilted back and forth in full examination mode.

"Bob Ross, eat your heart out. Paintbrush dropped."

A few moments later Sashmo walked out of his cave. The stars shined brightly over the Loch and the reflection hit him in the eyes causing him to squint harshly. His fur was still partly soaked from Ellie's spraying.

"Come here J.D," Sashmo said.

J.D. came scampering out of the cave. Sashmo bent down and began petting his hideous pet.

"DID I JUST PAINT THAT MASTERPIECE FOR NOTHING?" screamed Ellie. "You obviously don't expect the Hydra to take you seriously. Do you understand that the Hydra is, for all intents and purposes, the ruler of the mythical creatures now? And you're going to go down to your first Council meeting looking like a ragamuffin?" He changed his tone from anger to inquisitiveness, "And am I supposed to feed that thing while you're gone?" said Ellie, pointing at J.D.

Sashmo cocked his head sideways and stared at Ellie. He then sighed heavily and shook his entire body like a dog, soaking Ellie with water in the process. His brilliantly brown fur coat came out looking fluffy and perfect.

"That better? And No. He'll just find some trash here and there. He'll be fine," said Sashmo.

"Makes sense. I guess that is all he had to eat in New Jersey anyway," smirked Ellie.

J.D. snarled at Ellie.

"Just make sure he doesn't go off on a pillaging rampage again," said Sashmo.

"So I AM babysitting," Ellie said under his breath.

Sashmo turned around and kneeled down again to talk to J.D.

"Isn't that right boy? Good boy!"

Ellie put two fingers in his mouth and began to make a gagging noise. Before Sashmo could make a comment to Ellie's gesture, a giant creature flew in from the distance. It was their friend, Scotty. He is a quick-talking griffin with large wings, the head of an eagle and the body of a lion. He is widely known for hardly letting anyone else get a word out.

"Hey Scotty," Ellie said.

"Hey, hey, hey guys! You ready for the big mythical creatures Council meeting this year Sashmo? Big shoes to fill for ya. Sakeamo is the only Sasquatch to represent the Sasquatches since 'Never Seen, Never Bother.' Now, boom here you come. Sash to the Mo. Man you guys live forever. My condolences obviously." Quick to change the subject after putting his foot in his mouth, Scotty spotted J.D. "How's your freak of nature?"

"He's doing-," Sashmo started to respond. Scotty did not give him a chance to finish.

"It is supposed to be a good one this year! Wow, he is ugly. There's not supposed to be a lot of problems this year. That's what I hear from the pixies anyway. Is that miscreation going to eat me? Because he is salivating. Unlike last year where they had that whole Elf versus Brownies thing and the gargoyles didn't like how they were portrayed in human films. Blah, blah, blah."

"I think-," Sashmo tried to respond again.

At this point Ellie realized that this could go on for hours and turned around to walk towards his lake.

"Those guys act like the Hydra is actually going to do anything about it. You know how it is, 'Never seen, Never bother.' It's pretty ridiculous sometimes. All the hiding and whatnot. Travel by darkness. You should really get that thing looked at, maybe a nose job. Well the sun has set so I'm ready to take off when you are big guy. Hey, where'd Ellie go?"

"Back here buddy, I just needed to refresh my scales. They were getting-,"

Ellie tried to make up an excuse as to why he walked away, but for once, Scotty's ability to interrupt finally came in handy.

"Oh hey. Didn't see you slip away there. How ya been? I haven't seen you since that trip down to Atlantis," said Scotty.

"Good. Good. Okay, you guys have a ball. I'll be right here in my lake with that lovely spectacle of the animal kingdom. By the way, you think while you guys are out you could keep your eyes open for any VHS tapes of Bob Ross?"

Sashmo tilted his head in pure confusion. Scotty gestured to respond to Ellie's request but even he was speechless.

"What? I'm trying to paint a friendlier world," Ellie said responding to their gestures.

"Yeah, okay Ellie, see ya later," said Sashmo.

Sashmo petted J.D. one last time to say goodbye. He grabbed onto Scotty's wing and pulled himself onto his back. His large legs straddled over the winged beast. Sashmo waved goodbye to his two closest friends as Scotty's wings began to flap. His massive wings tore through the sky with a fierce velocity. The wind caused a ripple across the Loch and soon Sashmo and Scotty were lifted up into the air. They sailed off into the night sky.

Chapter Two: Abby

As the sun began to rise, Sashmo and Scotty flew high above a thick-canopied forest. The trees below were lush and green. Wild flowers grew out of control as it appeared this land had never been seen or touched by man. The wind was blowing Sashmo's fur back all the while Scotty is talking. Thankfully the wind was too loud for Sashmo to make out anything he was saying.

Scotty started to descend near a small opening in the forest. He opened his wings and glided down to the ground. Right in front of them was a large rock formation in the shape of a fountain. Vines covered it entirely. The clearest water Sashmo had ever seen flowed gently out of the top of it at a steady pace. Sashmo jumped off of Scotty's back and stared at the water in awe.

"Here we are. Beautiful right?" asked Scotty.

"It's stunning. But where is everyone?" asked Sashmo.

"Great question my friend. The local Jackalopes have gotten everything ready for the big meeting today."

Scotty walked to the wall of the fountain and stared intently. After a moment of feeling around, he picked a spot and knocked three times with a slight pause after the first knock. He put his ear to the wall and waited. After a moment, the same pattern of knocks was returned back to Scotty. Scotty stepped back from the wall and hunched over to stretch.

Sashmo could not help but to ask, "What are y-?"

"Shhhhh!" responded Scotty.

Scotty walked over to a tree and grabbed a stick. He then began to hum an Irish sounding hymn. He twirled the stick in his right hand and clicked his heals while bouncing around doing a dance. This lasted for about thirty seconds and it was the most absurd thing Sashmo had ever witnessed, a Griffin doing the Irish jig. Sashmo laughed uncontrollably. His laughter was broken once Scotty finished and an unforeseen door opened in the floor just in front of the fountain. The entrance led to a dark hallway of stairs.

"Laughing?" Scotty asked. "I've been working on that for weeks! I mean there was that one part where I jagged instead of jigged and my rhythm was a tad bit suspect, but it worked. I'm quite the dancer you know. Here a ball change, there a moonwalk, everywhere a heel turn."

Sashmo had no response for Scotty's rendition of "Old MacDonald". He simply shook his head as the two proceeded down the staircase.

The stairway descended three flights and opened into a grand hallway with a stunning lobby. Golden chandeliers with brilliant crystals lit up the room. There were large paintings of other mythical creatures lining the walls. Sashmo paused a moment as he noticed a picture of his grandfather Sagamo. He appeared visibly shaken, as he stared at the picture letting out a deep sigh.

The floor was set with the whitest marble he had ever seen. Its color reminded him of Abby. In the middle of the lobby sat a beautiful granite fountain, a smaller version of the one they were under with the same perfectly clear water. Around the room were a myriad of other mythical creatures who were attending the convention.

Sashmo scanned the room and saw leprechauns, mermaids, trolls, dragons, goblins, fairies, pixies, banshees, vampires, gremlins, centaurs, a minotaur, elves and a variety of creatures that appeared human.

Hugin and Munin were perched at a table. The messenger ravens of the Mythical Creatures were providing an update to all those around.

"Gather around, gather around," cawed Hugin.

"First report," said Munin.

"First report, first report," interrupted Hugin.

"If you allow me to please continue Hugin," said Munin.

"Continue, please continue," said Hugin.

Clearing his throat, Munin began again, "Issues facing the Council this year begin with Goblins and Trolls debating who has the right to reside under bridges. If you ask me, it should be water."

"Goblins and Trolls, Goblins and Trolls."

Munin threw his wings up in disgust.

"Moving on," yelled Munin.

"Next story, next story."

Sashmo had had enough. He had only one thing on his mind and listening to the two ravens argue through the news was not it. He eventually meandered to an opening in the crowd and he saw her. It was Abby.

Her fur coat was an impeccable white. She was as tall and beastly as he. Sashmo's heart skipped a beat at the sight of her. He took his first step to greet her when he stumbled into one of the human-looking creatures.

"Watch where ya going Bigfoot!" snarled the smaller beast in his snarky voice.

"What did you call me?" Sashmo said.

"I didn't stutter. Bigfoot."

The being began to encircle Sashmo. It looked him up and down as if he was his next meal. Sashmo was not sure how to act and began to cower away when Scotty approached.

"Hey there guys! What's up Jacob? Man, you werewolves really do look like humans. Gets me every time. Is there a moon tonight? Hey, would you still change even though you're underground? I've never seen a werewolf change before. Let me know if you do. What do you think they'll have at the banquet tonight? Hey Sash, good thing you're here. Guess who I saw? You guessed it, Abby. She's looking good buddy. You asked her out yet? What's the deal?"

"Does he ever shut up?" Jacob asked.

22

"Who Sashmo?" Scotty said. "No way. He's a talker man. Talk, talk, talk. You should see how ugly his pet is though. Kind of burns your eyes a bit."

Jacob grunted in a frustrating manner. "You're lucky this time Bigfoot."

"Lucky? Sash, did you win a door prize? What was it? A blindfold so you don't have to look at your pet anymore? Or was it a back scratcher? That'd be sweet."

"No Scotty," answered Sashmo.

Scotty started to open his mouth again to ask more questions when Abby approached them both.

"Weren't going to say hi Sashmo?" Abby asked.

"What happened was-"

Scotty cut Sashmo off, "Of course he was. Why wouldn't he? You're the only reason he came today. Do you smell pastries? Buffet must be ready."

Scotty lifted his nose in the air and walked away following the smell. Sashmo was clearly mortified as his shoulders and head dropped.

"Only reason?" Abby said in disbelief.

"Well, no. I mean kind of, maybe. No. Definitely not."

"I better not be. Taking your father's seat amongst the representatives should be an honor Sashmo. Your family and their deeds echo throughout the history of the Council."

"It's not that-" Sashmo said.

23

"Smooth as always Sash. I need to go. I'm speaking in front of the Council tonight."

"Speaking? About what?"

"Don't worry about it."

"But I do worry."

"Do you?"

Before Sashmo could respond, Abby turned and walked away. With nothing but her back facing him and nothing to say, Sashmo just stood there. The feeling of shame and regret the only things to keep him company.

Chapter Three: The Convention

Sashmo sauntered through a lavish door into a grand room. Another giant chandelier hung from the ceiling, lighting up the room as bright as the northern lights. A large oval table sat in the middle of the room. The other mythical creatures that serve on the Council had already gathered and found their seats. Another assortment of creatures filled the audience within the room in stadium style seating. The smaller creatures were seated nearest to the front, while the large beasts filled up the back and the sides.

Sashmo, already late, meandered his way through the aisles to find his seat at the floor table. His seat just so happened to be near the front on the furthest side from the entrance. He was forced to go all the way through the crowd and completely around the table to reach it. As he lumbered through the crowd, he felt the stinging gaze of all the creatures watching him. As he embarrassingly tried to make his way, the Hydra saw that it was Sashmo. The Hydra stood up and everyone immediately became silent. Sashmo stopped and noticed all ten of the Hydra's eyes on him. The Hydra's gaze felt like they were piercing his soul. After a moment of extremely awkward silence, the Hydra began clapping. It took a moment for the rest of the creatures to join in. Sashmo was suddenly receiving a standing ovation.

Sashmo was humbled. He threw a hand up, waived, and walked to his seat. He knew that this was where his father and grandfather had sat during Council. The feeling of honor changed quickly to a feeling of embarrassment and pain. He turned to give one more wave and then sat down.

A large Ogre walked to the front of the room and stood behind the Hydra. He pulled a large mallet from tucked inside his belt and slammed it against the table.

"SILENCE!" Yelled the Ogre. "This here meeting is now under se- se- session!"

The Hydra whose five heads are named Alpha, Beta, Delta, Epsilon and Gamma stood up and began to address the Council.

Alpha started, "In the names of the brothers and sisters whom have come before us, we do hereby ordain this the 2361st Council of the Mythical Creatures now in session."

"Never seen, never bother!" followed Beta.

All the mythical creatures repeated, "Never seen, never bother."

Sashmo was very confused by all of the pomp and circumstance. He had attended many of these meetings as a child but he never paid that much attention. In what was a weak attempt to seem like he knew what is going on, he muttered "Never seen, never bother" a second later than everyone else. This brought a few condescending glares from creatures nearby.

The Hydra continued to stand, Gamma began to speak, "Because it is a rare occasion for a representative to be replaced, especially one that held such high authority, let the record show that I would like to start this meeting off by personally welcoming Sashmo the Sasquatch. We are all excited that you were able to make the trip."

"Here, here!" The Council responded.

Alpha continued, "Your father, Sakemo, was an outstanding leading member of this Council. He helped pave the way for many things that the Council and mythical creatures everywhere stand for today. He was also a dear friend of mine. That, combined with the great sacrifice of your grandfather, means that your voice is always welcome here. Is there anything you want to say before we begin normal proceedings?"

Sashmo stood up, "Yeah, umm... Thanks. Should I have brought a scepter?"

Abby, who was sitting a few seats away, rolled her eyes. Sashmo, obviously embarrassed about his comment, simply gave a nod to the Hydra and sat back down.

Beta began the meeting, "Before we get to the usual phase of old business, it was brought to my attention that we have a special request to bring an issue before the Council by the Yeti representative, Abigail Abominae. Miss Abominae, please step forward and state your issue."

Abby stood and walked in front of the Hydra. She took her place a podium before him. As this was an unusual request, all the representatives were silent and in suspense.

"Your high command, I come before you today in desperate need of your help. The humans have set plans to begin drilling for oil in our home. If they begin, there is no way we would be able to stay where we are. It has been our home for generations. Without the frozen tundra our species would be unable to survive."

There was an uproar from the crowd.

"Silence!" exclaimed Beta. "What of a migration to a region in Antarctica?"

Ymir of the Ice Giants, a giant bald-headed beast stood up. His skin was solid white. His face carried years of worry and pain, as well as a frozen beard. Icicles protruded from his head, giving the illusion of hair. His height was well above Sashmo's and it was as though he had a permanent scowl for an expression.

"The Ice Giants are having a hard enough time as it is in Antarctica. We have been forced to become semi-nomadic in our search for food there. We do not need an entire race of Yetis invading and competing for survival. I believe that a migration there would be the end of both our species."

"Then there is nothing we can do," said Gamma.

There was another uproar from the delegates.

Abby cried out, "But we will become extinct!"

"We must listen to other suggestions," said Epsilon.

The representative for the Goblins stood up. "Let's unite and take out the humans once and for all! Together we would have the ability for the mythical creatures to be the dominant group of species on this planet! First it was Sagamo, then the Amazon Women. Even the Hobbits were lucky to escape alive. When will this end? Where do we draw the line?"

The fever pitch of the crowd reached its highest point yet.

"I will second that motion," said the Leprechaun representative, "we have been living in hiding for long enough!"

Even though there was a loud discordance, everyone seemed to cheer after the Leprechaun spoke.

"You are proposing an all-out war against humans. You understand that this means one extinction of a species to save another?" questioned Alpha. "If that is the way the delegates feel; we should put it to a vote."

"Whoa now," Jacob, the representative for werewolves stood up. "Let's not be too hasty here. What about the code?"

A Centaur, sitting next to Jacob stood up to respond. "There was once a time for the code. This be a call to arms!"

The representatives mounted another major uproar. Jacob, with a look of confusion, thought for a moment and then opened his mouth for a rebuttal of the call to arms. Right as he was about to speak, a deep resonating voice towered over the entire congregation.

"You can try. The humans are too powerful. We, the Stone Giants, were once the dominant race on Earth. We ruled kingdoms near and far. Then the humans came along. They multiplied and developed weapons and wits. Their technology created things we were no match for. Wars raged and now but a few of us remain."

It was a different time then. The truce didn't come along between creatures and humans until many years after the Stone Giant Wars. Odus, the King of the Ice Giants, had seen his people decimated by man. Though he supported the truce when it was negotiated, he had always been a strong supporter of Sakemo and the Hydra's evolution of the Council to the policy of "never seen, never bother."

The Centaur, still standing responded, "Together, we must fight!"

"And you will lose," rebutted Odus. "Your best bet is appeasement to prolong the mythical creature world for as long as possible."

The entire room fell silent and waited for the high Council of the Hydra to deliberate.

After a few moments, Epsilon said, "Due to the important nature of this issue, we have decided the correct action. The Centaurs are right about one thing. There was once a time for the code. The code was put into place to protect all mythical creatures from the short-sightedness of the humans. Sakemo and I decided that going into hiding and living our lives under the radar of the humans was our best chance of survival until something changed. It is still the time for that very same code. So our decision, with a heavy heart Miss Abominae, is to adapt. We cannot and will not fight."

"But-" pleaded Abby.

"No buts," Beta said, "Never seen, never bother. It is how it is and always will be. In accordance with the Stone Giant's testimony, this rule was formed to protect us all. No exceptions can be made for a single species. The casualties would far outweigh the reward. We must think for the greater good. You are dismissed Miss Abominae."

Tears flowed down Abby's icy fur. They chilled and turned to ice before falling off her face. Abby stormed out of the conference room as everyone watched silently. The door slammed and for a moment no one knew how to break the silence. In utter disbelief of what just happened at his first Mythical Creatures Council meeting, Sashmo stood up, shook his head and dismissed himself from the room as well.

Sashmo's disruption opened the window for the high Council to move the meeting forward. "We must move on. We will now hear arguments from Golash the Goblin about whether Trolls or Goblins have the right to nest underneath bridges," Delta said.

Sashmo caught up to Abby outside the meeting room. "Abby, wait."

"There's nothing for you to do Sashmo."

"I… I could try."

"You're sweet Sash, you know you are. We both know you're not exactly the hero type though."

Sashmo was so hurt he could not muster up any words. He did what came naturally to him and hung his head in shame.

"There's nothing left to do. The Council was our only option. Don't worry yourself with it Sash." Abby turned, walked away and left the chamber.

"But I love you Abby…"

Chapter Four: The Plan

A couple days later, back at Loch Ness, the stars shined and gentle breeze blew across the lake. Ellie and J.D. were on the water front. Ellie was throwing a large whale bone off in the distance and J.D. retrieved it multiple times. The bone was heavy. It took Ellie a good crow-hop to get it far enough to interest J.D.

"Okay JD, last time, let's see what you got," said Ellie.

With both hands, Ellie took a massive hop, let out a hefty grunt and launched the bone into the air. J.D. did a slight jab step as if he was going to track the bone down, but stopped. Just like a skeet shooter, as the bone flew through the air, J.D. took a deep breath and shot a ball of fire at the bone. The flame hit the bone perfectly as it flew through the air. Nothing but ashes floated down to the ground.

Ellie was amazed. He had never seen J.D. display this trait before, "Wow. That's new. And in no way can I see this new skill being used poorly in the future. Once Sashy gets back, that's his problem. GOOD BOY!"

J.D. heard those two magical words and scampered back over to Ellie. J.D. began to lick Ellie uncontrollably, his excitement bubbled over in playful love. He jumped onto Ellie's chest and knocked him over. Ellie appeared to be having a good time when he started to hear a constant rambling coming from the skies. Sashmo and Scotty had returned.

"Ugh! Get away from me J.D.! You're such a pest!" Said Ellie.

He placed his tail on J.D.'s head in order to keep him back. J.D. gave Ellie an inquisitive look and did not understand as his legs simply ran in place. As Scotty and Sashmo landed behind Ellie, he turned and acted as though he didn't see them coming.

"Oh hey guys. You snuck up on me. How did everything go?"

Scotty beat Sashmo to respond as usual, "It was great! Great buffet. Saw some old friends. Soft batch cookies. Yum in my belly!"

J.D. caught Scotty's eyes.

"That thing hasn't been summoned back to the underworld yet? Hades must be missing him. Well I would love to stay and chat but I have to get back before any humans notice a statue missing."

Sashmo stood quietly for a moment as if he was in a different world. His mind was clearly elsewhere as even Scotty's ramblings didn't detour him from his trance. His face hung with a melancholy look.

"Alright. See ya later Scotty," replied Ellie. Ellie then proceeded to hit Sashmo with his elbow to get him to come to.

A startled Sashmo shook his head and realized what was happening.

"Yeah, thanks again Scotty. See ya next year."

He then turned and moped towards his cave. J.D. was so happy to see Sashmo that he licked him, jumped on him and nuzzled his head against Sashmo's knee. Sashmo did not pay him the slightest bit of attention. Ellie knew what was wrong and waddled to catch up.

"Went that well eh Sash?"

"Is it that obvious?"

"What happened this time? It wasn't worse than that time we tried to build a man cave in Wiltshire was it?"

"No. It's not that. Abby spoke before the Council and the Hydra. Humans are drilling for oil where her and her clan live. They are being driven from their homes and there's nowhere to go."

"The Council won't help I assume."

"You know how it is. Never seen, never bother."

"You know what it means if that five-headed mongrel won't do anything right?"

"I'm going to lose the love of my life? I'll never have children?" Wait, my life has no meaning?"

"No, no and no! I mean no, no and yes. Or yes, no yes. You know what I mean. It means that if the Council won't do anything, maybe you should. It's time to show Abby what you're made of. Seven hundred pounds of pure, furry beast."

"I'm not sure 'furry' works there Ellie."

"Hispid? No. Chaetophorous sounds pompous. Bristly. Pure, bristly beast."

J.D. got excited, his tongue hung low and he began circling Sashmo and Ellie in the air.

35

Sashmo briefly imagined the possibility of doing something to save Abby. Then the reality of Ellie's plan sank into his mind.

"Okay, so as much as I have always dreamed of being a vigilante, it's in Alaska," said Sashmo.

"Sarcasm noted, but if my great, great grandfather, Lotan the Leviathan, can roam the entire ocean, I think we can make it to Alaska."

Sashmo perked up a bit with a skeptical grin on his face, "Your great, great grandfather was a Leviathan?"

"Size sometimes skips generations!" Ellie said defensively. "Not the point. We need to get those low-life humans outta there. I think I have a plan. To get there anyway. We can wing the rest. What's the worst that could happen?"

Sashmo's passive nature kicked in after Ellie's question. He began to envision the worst things that could happen to them. Ellie had a history of bad ideas dating back as long as Sashmo could remember. Sashmo imagined himself inside a cage as part of a traveling circus. Lion tamers were ordering him to jump through flaming hoops as they violently cracked their whip at him. Children's faces in the crowd lit up with excitement as the ring announcer referred to him as the 'The Great Bigfoot.' Ellie was there too, walking the tight rope behind him, balancing himself with a long wooden pole as the crowd cheered wildly.

Sashmo shook his head as a second vision came to him.

An Eskimo stood proudly in front of a fire place. The living room of his log cabin was illuminated by the fire. There was a beautiful polar bear rug covering the hardwood floors. Above the fire place, Sashmo, Ellie and J.D.'s heads were mounted.

"Ahh!' screamed a startled Sashmo as he brought himself back to reality.

The Council has drilled the code into the minds of the mythical creatures. Getting caught by the humans was known to come with the severest of punishments. The exact extinct of which were however unknown. The only way for the code to be effective is for all the creatures to follow. The potential of these punishments served as effective deterrents. The safety of mythical creatures depended on the ongoing evaporation of their existence from the memory of humans. The "legends" that existed to man keep them from hunting them down or looking for any creatures. If any creature broke the code, then all creatures would be in danger. The exact conditions or consequences for getting caught were unknown to Sashmo but that is not even something he wanted to imagine.

The second image in Sashmo's mind almost made him put his foot down. Ellie would not put a stop to his plans otherwise. He came out of his daze and saw Ellie and J.D. Then he turned to look at his cave and Loch Ness.

"Right. Worst that could happen. Can't be any worse than going extinct. I think."

"That's the spirit," said Ellie. "Now grab your things. It's getting dark. I need to grab my fanny pack. Then we can get moving."

Sashmo, Ellie and J.D. walked through the forest for about an hour. It was dark out when they came to a ledge with a clearing down below. Everything was lit by the light of the half moon. The clearing contained a series of white storage buildings with green roofs. The entire area was surrounded by a chain link fence.

"We're here. This is the place," Ellie whispered.

The trio walked down to the fence line. Sashmo looked over his shoulder every three seconds, constantly suspicious of getting caught or being exposed. Ellie pulled a pair of wire cutters out of his fanny pack and began to cut through the fence. The sound of cutting metal is unmistakable and rattled Sashmo even more.

"Hurry up Ellie," said Sashmo.

"Will you calm down?"

Ellie finished cutting through the chain links of the fence. Sashmo and Ellie walked through the hole. J.D. was already waiting on the other side as he had simply flown over.

"Thanks for the help J.D. Real team player," Ellie said snidely.

Ellie motioned the others to follow him. They walked up to one of the storage units with a pad lock on the door. Ellie dug through his fanny pack and pulled out more tools. He started to pick the lock, making discernible noise.

"You can't do that any faster?" Sashmo said as his nerves were slowly starting to take him over.

"Why are you getting so bent out of shape?" Ellie snapped back as he continued to work. "We spend our entire lives hiding from humans. We are good at it. This place just has slightly more traffic. A little bit more of a challenge. If you care about Abby-"

"Okay, okay," Sashmo said realizing they needed to stick to the plan. "How do you even know how to do that?"

"I used to date this Harpy. She was always stealing stuff."

A moment later the lock opened. Ellie again motioned to Sashmo and J.D. to follow him. They went inside the building where there was no light.

"I can't see anything," said Sashmo.

"J.D., give us some light," whispered Ellie.

J.D. inhaled slightly and breathed a small flame, about the size of a candle

"Since when? How did you?" Sashmo began.

"I'll explain later. Carry this. J.D. put this on your back. I got this. We're good. Let's go," Ellie said.

The three of them, all carrying their designated pieces, left the building, shimmied back through the fence and headed back into the forest.

Chapter Five: The Kraken

The next day, the sun was shining. A clear blue sky provided it with a picturesque backdrop. There was a gentle breeze blowing west and the three friends of Sashmo, Ellie and J.D. were cramped in a basket, hovering across the Atlantic Ocean under a red and blue hot air balloon. J.D. was all but out of breath from breathing fire into the balloon. With each forceful breath he looked a bit more exhausted. As he looked at his companions he knew he must keep it up. The basket drifted just barely above the ocean surface, occasionally dipping down and hitting the water. Ellie used his long neck to suck up water and then spew it out in a stream, helping to propel the vessel. Sashmo stood with his arms crossed, perplexed as to how he let Ellie talk him into such a ridiculous circumstance.

"So this was your great plan?"

"I didn't see you coming up with any genius ideas. I didn't calculate for your 700 pounds and 'Odin's-sense-of-humor's' pixie lungs."

Sashmo wiggled around and turned in disgust. Ellie leaned over to suck up another load of water when the seas beneath them begin to quiver. At first the quiver seemed to be mild, perhaps even normal. However, the shaking water became progressively more violent. Sashmo and Ellie turned to look at each other, both with scared and confused looks on their faces.

The water sank under beneath them. They suddenly became a skyscraper's length above the water when an enormous, dark, scaly beast rose from below. It was ten times larger than the balloon and resembled a squid. It had a mouth that contained countless rows of very sharp teeth. At least twelve tentacles were the above water's surface. The creature's body was covered in scars.

Sashmo, Ellie and J.D. huddled together, much tighter than before when the beast opened its mouth. It began to unlock its jaw like a snake and let out a deafening roar. The squid-like creature leaned over, mouth open, to devour the balloon and its passengers. Right before it was about to inhale the balloon, the enormous creature opened its eyes and saw the ghostly white threesome.

"Ellie! I Didn't know that was you. What's happening buddy?" said the Beast.

Ellie heard his name and peeked his head around Sashmo.

"Kraken! You almost gave me a heart attack. Three hundred and thirty-six is way too young to die. I still have my best years ahead of me,"

Sashmo nudged Ellie. His face was still blank with fear.

"Oh. Krakey here is my eighth cousin, five times removed or something. His great aunt is 2nd cousins with my dad's brother's wife's aunt's niece," said Ellie.

"You just made that up."

"Tomato, asparagus buddy. The important thing is that we didn't get eaten."

41

"So whatcha doing all the way out here?" asked the Kraken.

"As it just so happens, we are questing," replied Ellie.

"Yeah? What's this quest about? And what's with that unsightly boar looking thing you got there?" asked Kraken.

Sashmo petted J.D. He's used to hearing these type of things. The affection was still very much appreciated.

"My good buddy Sashmo here is trying to go save a Yeti-friend. He thinks she is the bee's knees."

Sashmo, still afraid of getting caught, hit Ellie in the shoulder.

"What? The 20's slang isn't working for me? Always been my favorite era of the humans" said Ellie. "Oh, oh, oh. It's fine. Kraken is blood."

"A Yeti huh? Love the white fur. Reminds me of the snow-capped mountains of Olympus. So innocent," said Kraken.

"She is pretty special," Sashmo responded.

"Yeah, yeah special. Sounds like love to me," said Kraken.

"You bet your tentacles on it," said Ellie.

Kraken's eyes squinted and he let out a deep sigh, "I know a lot about love. I've seen it, centuries and centuries of it. It is the only thing that makes watching the human world bearable. All those wars. Pain., lies, and hate. Made me want to dive deep down into the water and never poke my head above the surface again. But when I see the way that mankind loves, you could search the farthest ends of the universe and not find anything so beautiful. So yes, I know that love is unconditional. But I also know that it can be unpredictable,

42

unexpected, uncontrollable, unbearable and strangely easy to mistake for loathing and… What I'm trying to say is love makes you do crazy things. So yeah, quest along boys."

Sashmo and Ellie were at a loss of words. The sudden emotional depth of the Kraken had surprised them.

"Wow," Sashmo said breaking the awkward silence.

"See? That's what I've been saying Sashmo," said Ellie.

"That's not even close to what you have been saying Ellie."

"Yeah, yeah. I'll let you guys be on your way. It was good seeing you Ellie. Take care. If you need anything, you know where to find me," said Kraken.

"Actually I don't," responded Ellie.

"You'll figure it out. See ya later."

Kraken swam around the other side of the balloon. He took a deep breath and blew the hot air balloon far into the distance. The wind created by Kraken was strong but not swift. The balloon tossed and turned as it flew through the air. Sashmo, Ellie and J.D. screamed as the balloon tumbled its way into the distance.

Chapter Six: Shangri-La

"The quest has begun Lilianna," said the Fairy Oracle.

The Oracle is a green-skinned fairy about the size of a thumb. She was wrapped in white cloths with translucent wings protruding from her back. Her piercing blue eyes have the ability see into a creature's soul.

The Oracle lives in the palace at Shangri-La. The palace gates are protected by the Unicorn Guard; an ancient line of Unicorn warriors whose singular purpose is to protect the Fairy Oracle. The Oracle sits on a throne made from a branch of the mythical Tree of Knowledge that is carved into an owl. The owl's wings protrude to form the arms of the throne. At the end of each arm sit two carved hummingbirds.

The Oracle is a prophetic fairy that has existed as long as creation. She can see all outcomes. All possible scenarios. All potential events. There are but a few moments in history that the Oracle has found that there was only one path that could be allowed. It is questionable at best to play with fate. Destiny is a funny thing. It has a way of wanting to play itself out along the natural course of events. However, the Oracle knows the rules of destiny and works to ensure only the most important of outcomes.

Fairies have always been the overseers of the mythical creature world. They fly to where they are needed, observe and report back to the proper creatures. When fairies need advice on how to move forward on a particular issue, they seek council with the Oracle.

Lilianna is a yellow-skinned fairy that had been summoned. She was a young fairy who had experienced very little in her time of duty. She was draped in light orange cloths with golden hair half way down her back. She wore a necklace made of hemp with multiple anklets to match. Her wings were much smaller than that of the Oracle but resembled those of a monarch butterfly.

"I hate to question you your highness, but are you sure about this Sasquatch?" asked Lilianna.

"All you know is prima facie. Creatures do not realize their full potential until a dramatic event calls for them to. Such as something they love being put into danger. It's only that catalyst that allows their greatness to rise to the surface. Sashmo the Sasquatch is now in a position to become the most vital mythical creature for generations to follow. This is of the highest importance," answered the Oracle.

"I just don't see it," replied Lilianna.

"You are young Lilianna. This too is your time to shine. Understand that we do not have to understand why the gods make their decisions. When Sashmo's grandfather, Sagamo, sacrificed his life to save the Hydra, that sacrifice echoed through the generations. That sacrifice gave Sashmo's father, Sakemo, the strength to move the Council and all mythical creatures in a new direction. It is too that which will push Sashmo to face the trials that lie before him."

"What must be done?" asked Lilianna.

"Guide his quest. Ensure that he finds his inner hero. Should he fail, his grandfather's bravery and sacrifice will never fill his heart and the destiny of his bloodline will not be complete. At this point there still are many outcomes to his quest. Sashmo must save Abigail Abominae. This task falls on your shoulders youngling. Be swift and effective. If he fails, all mythical creatures will be in grave danger."

"I won't let you down," Lilianna said. She left the throne room and went in search of Sashmo.

Chapter Seven: Canadians

The red and blue hot air balloon lied torn and shredded on the ground of a frozen landscape. Snow fell gently on the balloon. The basket was broken into several pieces. Ellie was sprawled out on the snow, face down. Sashmo laid much closer to the majority of the basket. He was barely conscious.

A small white rabbit hopped past Sashmo and began to investigate J.D. J.D.'s head was stuck in the snow like an ostrich. The bunny got closer and sniffed J.D. His smell caused the rabbit to turn its head in disgust. J.D. raised his head out of the snow, shook off the remaining flakes from his face and looked straight at the rabbit. The rabbit's eyes opened shockingly wide.   It let out a high pitched scream that would rival a banshee and fled into the forest. The scream aroused Sashmo.

"Ellie. You dead man?" asked Sashmo.

"Nope. Is J.D.?"

"Nope," said Sashmo.

"Unlucky."

Sashmo struggled to get to his feet and brushed himself off.

"So Captain my captain, where are wc?" asked Sashmo.

"Let me check my GPS," said Ellie.

"I assumed you would have one in your fanny pack," joked Sashmo.

"Somewhere cold?"

"Brilliant. So we have no clue where we are," said Sashmo..

"Yeah, but think of the adventure," said Ellie trying to brighten up Sashmo's mood.

J.D. began to yip and yap. He ran over to Sashmo and made a whining voice. Sashmo looked at him confused as J.D. dug his front hooves into the snow and yipped louder.

"Not now J.D. I'm not in the mood to play," said Sashmo more annoyed than before. "Your sarcasm is not helping Ellie."

"Think of Abby?" Ellie said trying to lighten the mood again.

"Yeah great, Abby. The Yetette of my dreams. She's out there being run off her home. Then here we are, in the middle of... somewhere."

"See? There ya go big guy. We are *somewhere*. I like the positivity."

J.D. ran back over to Sashmo and was howling uncontrollably. He jumped up and down on all four legs.

"J.D. stop!" yelled Sashmo.

J.D. stopped howling and jumping. He snarled harshly at Sashmo. J.D. turned, walked about ten feet away and launched a ball of fire at a sign. The fireball caused all the snow to melt off the sign and its words became readable.

Ellie began to laugh, "Well I'll be. You might be useful after all."

48

The sign read, "Welcome to Cartright, Newfoundland, Canada."

"I don't believe it. We made it across the ocean," said Sashmo in bewilderment.

"There ya go Sashy. Canada, America's hat."

"You do realize still how far away we are, right?"

"It's Canada. Can't be that big. You'd hear a lot more about it if it was."

Before Sashmo could relay to Ellie just how large Canada is, a gunshot rang out in the distance. Sashmo and Ellie turned and instinctively looked at one another while J.D. moved close to Sashmo. He stood alert with his ears perked up at full attention.

"What was that?" asked Sashmo fearfully.

"Oh it's probably just some humans. They like to shoot guns at cans for some reason," Ellie said.

"We should get out of here," said Sashmo more frantic than before.

"You don't think we should check that out?"

"And risk breaking the code? No."

Ellie gave Sashmo a nod of approval. The duo began to walk in the opposite direction of the shots when J.D. flew over their heads and landed in front of them. J.D.'s lip curled to one side.

"J.D. let's go. There's nothing but trouble that way," said Sashmo.

J.D. shook his head and dug his front right hoof into the ground, moving it back and forth like a bull.

"J.D. no," Sashmo tried again.

J.D. took in a deep breath and blew a line of fire, melting the snow and setting the ground ablaze. The look in his eyes dared Sashmo and Ellie to cross it.

"Smokey the Bear would be very disappointed in you," said Ellie.

"Okay fine. If we must. Put that out and stay here," replied Sashmo.

Sashmo walked to the nearby tree line and bumbled his way closer to where the gun shots rang out. A human's voice stopped him in his tracks. Sashmo peeked around a tree to see two men standing in a small makeshift campground. They both had rifles on their shoulders and were wearing white camouflage. One of the men was holding a glass jar.

"Jeb! I caugh' it. Right hur in me mason jar," said Stanley.

"Yous caugh' it eh? Look a'there. Ya did. Looks like quite the lil booger there," replied Jeb.

"Whatdoya think aboot that is there?" asked Jeb.

"No Idea Stan. But I's bet there's some money in it for ya."

Sashmo looked a little father around the tree to where he could see the mason jar. Inside was the yellow fairy Lilianna. She was breathing heavily as she tried to break the glass. Sashmo's eyes got big as he contemplated to himself what to do.

Sashmo began talking under his breath, "Okay Sash. Humans. Never seen, never bother. Wait. That little fairy is doomed if we don't try to save her. That's what Abby would do. Never seen, never bother. Mythical creature punishments. Ugh..."

"Why don' we just hunker down fer the night," said Stanley.

"You don' spose we should get her somewhere tonight?" Said Jeb.

"Wouldn' worry about it. What's that lil thing gonna do tonight that it wouldn' do in the mornin?"

Sashmo heard that the men were staying for the night so he scurried back to his friends. As Sashmo ran up, Ellie threw a stick to J.D. Instead of fetching it, J.D. shot fireballs at it. Sashmo caught them playing this time.

"Really Ellie?" Sashmo said.

"Yeah, I got nothing. What's the story with the gun shots?" Ellie asked.

"Nothing really. There's just these two hunters that-," Sashmo's voice begins to fade.

"Wait. What was that last bit Mumbly McMumblesome?"

"Maybe we should continue questing," replied Sashmo.

"No, no. The last part again."

"Oh you know Ellie, just run of the mill..." Sashmo's voice trailed off again.

"Mumbo jumbo is not one of the eight languages that I speak semi-fluently. But it sounded like you said there was a fairy trapped in a jar back there."

"WHAT?" Sashmo said acting as though that's not what he said.

"If that is true, I'm with you buddy. I dated a fairy once. Fairies be crazy," said Ellie.

"Alright, questing on," said Sashmo.

As Sashmo and Ellie turned to walk away, J.D. jumped in front of them standing in the same position as before. J.D. took in a deep breath when Sashmo stopped him.

"Okay, okay. We'll need a plan."

"Lucky for us I always have such good ones," Ellie said with an unwarranted confidence.

Chapter Eight: Saving Lilianna

Sashmo and Ellie waited until the dark. The two men's camp was set up with two tents side by side and a still-burning fire in front of them. Empty cans and other trash from their dinner were scattered about the site. One of the tents appeared to have a yellow light shining inside.   All was quiet when two heads poked out around the side of a tree.

"Okay, so just like we talked about, right?" Ellie said.

"Yup. Tom Cruise, Mission Impossible style," said Sashmo.

"Really? Cruise? I was thinking Sean Connery, Bond-style."

"If you want to go Bond, I like Daniel Craig."

"Ouch. My mother would cringe-"

"Okay. Fine. Focus. On three."

Sashmo handed Ellie a camouflage water bottle with the word "JEB'S" written in black marker on it. Ellie sucked down the contents of the bottle.

One, two…"

Right after the verbal "two" Ellie stretched his neck around the tree and sprayed the water into the camp putting out the fire.

"Should I be surprised?" Sashmo asked.

"Sorry. I got excited," replied Ellie.

Sashmo tip toed carefully to the tent with the yellow glow. He bent down and ever-so-carefully unzipped the tent flap. Inside slept

Jeb in his sleeping bag, the jar containing Lilianna tucked tightly underneath his arm.

Sashmo reached for the jar. He wiggled it just a bit. Lillianna sat inside the jar, visually weakened by her circumstance. As the jar moved slightly, Jeb stirred briefly and rolled over, still asleep. The jar was now more covered than before. Sashmo's eyes lit up as he had a plan. He grabbed a nearby stick and attempted to tickle Jeb enough to roll back over and loosen the jar.

J.D. spotted the stick from the tree line and ran into the camp site barking and howling. Jeb was startled awake and saw Sashmo and J.D. hovering outside his tent. Stanley came out of his tent and saw them as well. There was a moment of awkward silence as all four stared at each other. Confusion echoed inside of Stanley and Jeb's heads while fear consumed Sashmo and J.D. Simultaneously, all four let out screams. Ellie came darting into the mix as well.

"AHHH!! What are we screaming about?" asked Ellie.

The hunters reached in their tent to grab their guns. Jeb also grabbed Lilianna. J.D. flew off as Sashmo and Ellie took off through the woods. Jeb and Stanley were not far behind.

Sashmo and Ellie ran until they were both out of breath. They saw a large rock and ducked behind it. Both creatures bent over breathing heavily.

"I knew this was a bad idea, but of course I let you talk me into anyway," said Sashmo while he tried to catch his breath.

"Yeah, yeah. What about the fairy?" asked Ellie.

The two heard the hunters coming their way.

"I can't believe I'm saying this. Against my better judgement, we have to go back for her," said Sashmo.

"I'm sure somewhere in the mythical code book there is some exception to "Never seen, never bother, right? Like saving fairies?" Ellie asked.

"Doubt it buddy. You didn't see her struggling inside that jar though. Maybe sometimes you just have to do what's right. Follow my lead."

Sashmo and Ellie crept around to the other side of the rock. The forest was still lit by the half-moon but the jar Jeb carried was clearly visible. Sashmo squatted down to give the appearance he was hiding and motioned to Ellie to do the same. Ellie followed suit. Sashmo grabbed a handful of leaves and threw them on Ellie's back. He then did the same thing to himself. Sashmo let out a very weak-sounding roar.

"You hear that Stanley? Sounds like they hurt. This way," said Jeb.

Jeb and Stanley walked towards the rock that Sashmo and Ellie were beside. Jeb held up his makeshift lantern and saw the duo.

"There. They trying to be all in-con-spic-u-ous," said Jeb.

"What's that mean Jeb?"

"I don' know. I heard it on the Discovery."

Jeb pulled his rifle off his shoulder and pointed it at Sashmo. Sashmo and Ellie looked up at the men like deer in headlights.

"We got'em Stanley! How much ya think these two migh' be worth?" Jeb asked.

"More than that there lantern ya got there," replied Stanley.

At that moment, Sashmo stood up straight and tall with his chest bowed out. The two men hunched down and cowered backwards. Sashmo looked over to Ellie who was still clinging to the ground. He grabbed Ellie's flipper and pulled him up too. Ellie tried to mimic Sashmo's stance, although it was nowhere near as intimidating.

"Seems we have a little misunderstanding here gentlemen," said Sashmo in a deeper tone than his normal voice.

"Did yur jus' talk?" asked Jeb.

"Yes. Yes, I did. And that's because you are dreaming. Yup, none of this is real," said Sashmo as he casually waived his hands around in front of the two hunters.

"My dream or his?" asked Stanley.

"His?"

"Well I'll be there eh? How'd yous get in my dream Stanley?" Jeb said.

"Yur guess is as good as mine," said Stanley.

Jeb and Stanley continued to ramble on about dreams. Sashmo and Ellie noticed J.D. land in the branches above the two men. Ellie picked up a handful of debris from the forest floor.

"Okay guys. This has been fun and all but it's time to make it rain," said Ellie.

Ellie tossed the debris above the hunters' heads. J.D. could not resist and shot fire at all the leaves and sticks that caused a "rain of fire" to float down on the hunters. Jeb screamed, dropping the jar containing Lilianna. Sashmo dove out to grab the jar before it hit the ground. As Jeb and Stanley continued to try to swat away the burning ashes falling all around them, Sashmo, Ellie and J.D. took off through the woods once more.

The trio ran until they felt safe. All three were out of breath as they came to a clearing in the woods.

"Okay. I think we're in the clear. What now?" asked Sashmo.

"What do you mean 'what now'?" Ellie said. "Open it up."

Sashmo held the jar up. Lilianna was standing on the bottom of the jar with her hands on her hips. A vexing expression covered her face. Sashmo unscrewed the lid so Lilianna could float out. She began to hover as she crossed her arms.

"Are you okay?" asked Ellie.

"Yeah I'm fine. Those two weren't going to hurt me. Maybe sell me to the Lady of the Lake, but not hurt me," replied Lilianna.

"I thought the Lady of the Lake didn't make it?" asked Ellie.

"The rumor of her demise was put into place shortly after that whole thing went down. Once she gave Arthur the map to Excalibur, there were some words said. blah, blah, blah. She went back into the lake. Years later Sagamo was killed, then never seen, never bother, and she decides to fake her death. Made things easier. Since then she's become a bit of a collector and a recluse of sorts. Let's just say she dabbles in things that are really hard to find," replied Lilianna.

"Like maybe VHS cassettes of certain painters from the mid 1980's to the mid 1990's?" asked Ellie.

"What? No. I'm obviously talking about mythical objects."

"Right. Of course you are. Don't be silly. Moving on, I'm..."

"Ellie. That's Sashmo. And that thing is the Jersey Devil. Which is actually much uglier in person than I imagined," interrupted Lilianna.

Sashmo and Ellie stood with very confused looks on their faces.

"And just how?" Sashmo asked.

"You guys don't know?" Lilianna said.

The confused looks of Sashmo and Ellie failed to change.

"I'm a fairy." They still looked confused. Lilliana repeated in a slower voice, "I'm a fairy. Still nothing. Fairy. As in the overseer of mythical creatures. Our duty to the mythical creature world is to observe and report anything necessary to the proper creature. Perhaps the Hydra, the P.E.T., or the Oracle. Standing members of the Council should know that."

"First week on the job," said Sashmo.

"Who are the P.E.T.?" Ellie asked.

"This is going to be harder than I thought. Where have you been all of your adult life?" Lilianna asked.

"Loch Ness. In a cave," answered Sashmo.

Lilianna began to chuckle, "So literally under a rock?" She continued, "The P.E.T.s, Policing Extra Terrestrials. Don't call them 'pets'. If a fairy has to report to them, it is because a creature has broken the code. In which they would pick up the perp and do what they feel is an appropriate action."

"Oh, you said P.E.T.s. like with Droz and Tom. I knew that," Sashmo said confidently.

"Does that mean you're going to tell them about us?" asked Ellie.

"No. Why would I do that?"

"If you're truly an overseer, you must know our intentions," said Sashmo.

"I do. Sometimes things are more important than the code. Continue on your quest boys. I have nothing that is need of being reported."

"Umm. Okay. One last question. If you are magical and whatever, how come you couldn't get out of that jar?" asked Ellie.

Lilianna dropped her head. "The jar was small and my magic will bounce off of things if it there is an acute enough of an angle. It's like fiber optics where the light doesn't escape that strand because it is continuing to bounce...." Lilianna realized that she has completely gone over their heads in terms of science. "Glass is our weakness."

"Ohhhhhh," Sashmo and Ellie said simultaneously.

"Now go, time is of the essence" shouted Lilianna.

Sashmo grabbed J.D. by a horn and gently pulled him in one direction. Ellie began to walk to the opposite direction.

"It's this way Sash," said Ellie.

"I'm pretty sure it's this way buddy," replied Sashmo.

"I can settle this. Lilianna, which way is Alaska?" asked Ellie.

Lilianna pointed in a direction that neither one of them was walking.

"See? I was right, let's go," said Ellie.

Chapter Nine: Fenris

It was midday inside an office building. A young blonde-headed girl sat behind a desk answering phone calls. There was a large sign behind her that read, "Fenris Petroleum." The girl hung up the phone as a fax popped up behind her. She grabbed the fax and quickly ran it back to an office towards the back of the building. She entered the office and handed it to a middle-aged man wearing a suit with jet black hair and partial goatee.

"Mr. Williams. This just came in," said the girl.

Williams looked at the fax approvingly.

"Thank you. That will be all," said Williams.

The girl walked out and closed the door behind her. Williams opened a drawer of his desk. He reached his hand inside the top of the compartment and pulled down a secondary and hidden compartment. From inside the hidden drawer, he pulled out a phone and dialed a number.

"It just came in. The board approved it eight to one. The plan is going accordingly... I don't care... Who?... I still don't care. He doesn't mean anything to us now. Stick to the plan."

Williams hung up the phone and put it back in its secret location. He turned around to his bookcase, moved a few other books out of the way and grabbed a book that was hidden behind the main set of books on the shelf. The lone word on the cover was "Lunas." He flipped through a few pages. He suddenly came upon one that made him smile.

Williams looked down at his watch. He was running late. He marched through the office building and walked outside. There was a podium with a dozen reporters waiting, chatting amongst themselves. When Williams took the podium everyone became silent.

"The board has just approved our latest conquest for oil. We will begin the process shortly. The prospect of oil in Alaska is unimaginable," said Williams.

"Mr. Williams. What about the potential harm to wildlife?" One of the reporters asked.

"Good question. We specifically picked this region because there is no indigenous wildlife. The conditions there are too extreme. Mother nature never intended on life to grace this land. It was always meant for something more. Fenris Petroleum is dedicated to the conservation of the natural world. However, we must still do our due diligence to our shareholders."

"Mr. Williams. In that region this time of year, there is over two months of darkness. How will your men work?" Another reporter asked.

"That is correct. We will be working for the most-part when there is no sun. We can thank Thomas Edison for our ability to work. The drilling will commence in two weeks. No further questions."

Chapter Ten: Pillage

Sashmo and Ellie traveled across a snow covered field. Sashmo slushed up to his calf while Ellie's body was nearly fully-submerged. A snow covered forest towered over them in the distance.

"I'm cold," said Sashmo.

"Try being cold-blooded," replied Ellie.

"Why do we live at the Loch anyway?" asked Sashmo.

"That's where I was born. Then one day you just came roaming around there like a modern two-eyed Arimaspian. There was a sweet cave there and the rest is history."

"I get tired of ripping down signs with your picture on it. It never turns out right. They always put ears on you," said Sashmo.

"It is probably better that way," replied Ellie.

"When this is all said and done, me, you and old J.D. need to go somewhere tropical. I want little umbrellas in my drinks, brushing sand out of my fur…"

As Sashmo continued to ramble, Ellie looked behind him.

"Speaking of J.D., where is he?"

The duo looked around scouring the edge of the forest. Then they saw it, a cloud of smoke hurled into the air in the distance. Sashmo and Ellie turned to look at each other slowly. Ellie dropped his head before they began running in the direction of the smoke.

As they got closer to the origin of the smoke billowing into the air, their worst fear was realized. J.D. had gotten hungry and was now tearing apart livestock in a small village. Sashmo and Ellie crept up behind a shed. Looking out, they saw a small-town Main St. There were mom and pop shops with neighboring residential housing nearby that were covered in snow. It would have been a very peaceful scene if not for J.D.

J.D. was flying low to the ground. Fire was coming out of his nostrils. A chicken hung in his mouth, about to become his next meal. A group of angry villagers with pitchforks and shovels chased after him. The local villagers were shouting and screaming.

"Get it!"

"What is that thing?"

"That has to be the ugliest thing imaginable!"

"We have to get it! It's eating our chickens!"

"Yup, ugliest thing imaginable. That's all you had to say. Ugliest thing imaginable."

While the villagers were focused on J.D. flying above them, Sashmo and Ellie were able to creep up behind a building to get a closer look at the action.

"We've got to grab him," whispered Sashmo.

"We can't exactly just bust onto the scene and grab him. They have pitchforks," replied Ellie.

"Of all the dangers out there, you picked pitchforks?"

"I had a bad experience, okay?"

"You have any ideas?"

"Actually, I might," Ellie replied with a devious grin.

"I shouldn't have asked," said Sashmo.

As Sashmo and Ellie hatched their plan, J.D. spotted the villagers' cattle. His eyes grew wide and his tongue fell out of his mouth allowing the chicken to fall to the wayside. He began to salivate heavily as he flew straight towards the bull. Just as J.D. was about to pummel the unsuspecting beast, the bull whipped his horns around. His right horn smacked J.D. across the face and knocked him unconscious. The angry mob spotted their opportunity.

"Quick! Throw me the net!" yelled the leader of the mob.

A fellow mobber handed him an old fishing net and he threw it over J.D.

"Now, give me a pitchfork! This'll be the last time the ugliest thing imaginable messes with our chickens," the mob leader said.

"Wait!" said another member of the mob. "I's just spit-balling here but we's already got it trapped. Let's put it in a better trap. When it wakes up, it'll be alive and worth like hundreds of Canadian dollars eh."

"This thing is too powerful. Don't know anything in the whole village that could hold this beast," replied the leader.

"It burns my eyes just to look at it! Just get it over with! Ahhh!" came a scream from the back of the crowd.

"I think Ralphie back there is right. Best to be done with it," said the leader.

The leader of the mob raised the pitchfork high above his head. He was about to strike J.D.'s unconscious body. The crowd was silent as they all knew what was coming next. Then a loud voice using a 1930's transatlantic accent startled everyone.

"Excuse me, pardon me, excuse me here now," said Ellie.

"Eh," followed Sashmo in just a deeper voice than his normal one.

Ellie and Sashmo walked up to the crowd. They were disguised in things that they were able to find littered about the village. Ellie was wearing a skirt made of hay found in the chicken coop and wore a necktie made of orange marking tape off of the cow pasture fence. Sashmo had a fox fur on his head as a hat and a blanket around his shoulders found in a nearby shed.

"Let's hold on the impalement my friend," said Ellie.

"And just who does you be?" asked one of the villagers.

"We live on the outskirts of town. The important thing is we are here to help you out. Since you have led this expedition on capturing this exotic creature, you can make a lot of money," said Ellie.

"You mean like $400?" the mob leader asked with excitement.

"More than that my friend," replied Ellie.

"Eh," said Sashmo.

Ellie continued, "On my way walking up here I noticed that this creature is pretty large and is going to need a stronger cage to contain him."

66

"I think you're right Mr. We named it Ugliest Thing Imaginable or U.T.I. for short," said a villager.

"That's gross, but fitting. A great working title. It'll give people a burning sensation that they can't ignore. My colleague and I have the ability to tame wild creatures like this one. I am confident we can make it do whatever we want and you will reap endless profits. People will come from around the globe," replied Ellie.

During Ellie's rant, J.D. began to wake up and was extremely disoriented. He struggled to move but was trapped. He did the only thing he could; he let out a deafening shrieking noise.

"So you say you can tame that thing eh?" asked the leader.

"Eh," said Sashmo.

"Seeing is believing my friend," replied Ellie.

Ellie walked up to J.D. who is struggling to get free of the net, attempting to bite and claw his way out.

"Hey, it's me dummy," whispered Ellie. "Play along."

J.D. stopped struggling and his familiar dog-like smile came back across his face. Ellie pulled a stick out from under his skirt and waved it in the air.

"Here ya go boy," Ellie said as his manner of speak had turned to that of a hypnotist. "Is this what you want? Sit."

J.D sat up immediately. He was at full attention even with the net still draped over him.

"See that? Easy as pie. All you have to let me do is get him out of here, over to my place to put him in a proper cage and we can begin to set up an attraction of a lifetime," said Ellie.

"That's great! Let's do it!" said the leader.

As Ellie continued to speak with the villagers about the attraction they would create he was casually waving the stick in front of J.D. The Jersey Devil could resist no longer. J.D. took a deep breath and fire ignited out of his mouth, melting the strands of the net. Once free, J.D. bounded onto Ellie, knocked him over and grabbed the stick out of his mouth.

Between being trampled by J.D. and the fall, Ellie's necktie was ripped off and his skirt was torn to bits. After a moment of confusion, the leader of the mob gritted his teeth and clinched his pitchfork to the point of white knuckles.

"Oh no. Not the pitchfork. Run!" screamed Ellie.

Sashmo watched the leader of the mob run after Ellie. This scared him to the point of innately letting out a thunderous gorilla-like yell. Sashmo began running to catch up to Ellie and J.D. He passed the Canadian easily. During so, his disguise flew off as well.

"Get them!" the leader shouted.

After about thirty seconds of running through the snow, the leader looked back to see that his mob was not there. They were all ghostly white and shivered in fear.

"What are yous guys doing? Let's go," urged on the leader.

One of the members of the mob stepped forward very slowly and it is all she can do to simply shake her head "no." The leader sighed and dropped his head. He turned back around just in time to witness Sashmo, Ellie and J.D vanish into the woods.

Chapter Eleven: The Board Still Approves

A man in a grey suit was running across the street into an office building. He carried a briefcase in one hand and various rolled up charts and graphs under his other arm. Sweat dripped from his forehead. He had worried look on his face as he slipped through the front door of the building.

The man jumped on the elevator, pushed the button for the highest floor and waited anxiously. When the elevator finally opened, the logo for Fenris Petroleum caught his eye.

"Hello Mr. Dutch," said the blonde receptionist at the desk coming off the elevator.

"Is he angry?" asked Mr. Dutch.

"I'm sure he's not excited you're late, but they are expecting you," replied the girl.

Dutch hurried to walk past the receptionist desk and into a door behind it. He entered into a conference room that housed a long wooden table. Nine men sat around the desk, impatiently waiting for Dutch to arrive. Williams sat at the head of the table.

"I'm glad you could join us Mr. Dutch, as you are the board member who called the board meeting," said Williams.

"Yes sir. I apologize."

"You have five minutes. Begin."

Dutch took out the graphs and charts. He set up displays of them at the front of the table. He frantically opened up his briefcase and passed out various reports to all the men at the table.

"The reason I called this meeting is because I have been crunching the numbers. The data on the site in Alaska doesn't add up. As you can see in these reports, the drilling alone is going to cost Fenris ten billion dollars in the next five years alone. Unless a substantial oil find is actually made, nothing makes sense. No geologist believes that there is any oil near there. Most likely, Fenris will hemorrhage money until we are bankrupt. The eight of you approving this makes no sense at all."

Williams looked down at the paper work and began to nod his head.

"This is very impressive work Mr. Dutch," said Williams.

"Thank you sir," replied Dutch.

"However, while you were late, the board already decided to move forward, no matter what kind of data you brought here with you today," said Williams deviously.

"Sir, it's simply not logical. Stocks will plummet and shareholders will be enraged," said Dutch.

"This is about more than being logical," said Williams.

"Do you know something I don't?"

"There is a lot I know that you do not," said Williams.

Williams' eyes began to turn red. The other members of the board's eyes followed suit. Hair began to grow across each of their faces. Dutch's expression turned from anger to fear.

"Unfortunately for you Dutch, I know that you should have just kept being late."

Hair then began to grow on Williams' face until it was fully covered. His fingernails turned to sharp claws. His teeth slowly turned to fangs. Williams glanced at the half moon visible from the window and let out a thunderous howl. The other eight board members completed their transformations into werewolves as well. Williams pounced on Dutch taking him to the ground. The other werewolves joined. After only a few minutes the werewolves stood up. Their evil deed was done. The blood dripping down their mouths matched the red of their eyes. They began transforming back into their human form. There was a sudden knock on the door before it was flung open. There stood Jacob and his pack.

Jacob sees what remains of Dutch on the floor. "Looks like we just missed out on all the fun. C'mon boss!"

"Never mind that," said Williams. "Did all go well with that five-headed monstrosity?"

"Oh yeah. Huge buffet. Best food north of Agartha."

"Not that you imbecile. Did the Council decide to take action?"

"Oh right, just as you suspected. They stuck to the code."

"Excellent. That ignorant Hydra is incredibly predictable. Proceed with the plan, full force. There's nothing out there to stop us now."

Chapter Twelve: The Breakup

"That's it! I'm done!" Sashmo yelled at Ellie as they ran through the forest.

Sashmo, Ellie and J.D. ran until they were all out of breath. They soon arrived at a safe distance from the angry villagers. They finally came to a stop as Sashmo could not run any further. He propped all his weight up against a tree.

"I'm not doing this anymore," Sashmo said as he tried to catch his breath.

"Huh?" responded Ellie.

"J.D. and I are leaving. Back to my comfy cave at Loch Ness. This is all your fault. We have practically been caught by humans twice now thanks to you and your great ideas," Sashmo said.

"But Sashy, we've come so far."

"I don't care Ellie. It's over."

"Ohhh. I'm picking up what you're putting down. This is like a test to see if I'm going to throw in the towel and quit on you," said Ellie.

"No Ellie. No test, no games. I'm going home."

Sashmo turned and started walking in the direction from which they came. He whistled for J.D. J.D. somberly walked up behind Sashmo. He turned and looked back at Ellie with a sad expression on his face. Not even Ellie could deny how badly it made him feel.

After a brief moment, J.D. knew there was nothing that could be done and turned to catch up with Sashmo.

"Real funny Sash. How far are you going to walk to prove your point?"

Sashmo did not respond. He and J.D. walked further in the distance.

"Okay. Game, set, match. I'm sorry. You win," Ellie said. Then under his breath, "He'll be back, any second…"

Sashmo and J.D. continued through the semi-dense forest in silence. The cascading wind tickled the branches. Sashmo replayed the entire quest up to that point in his mind until he finally has to let it out.

"We don't need him J.D.," said Sashmo.

J.D. gave him a condescending look of 'yes we do.'

"Okay fine. Maybe you're right. Maybe I miss him already."

Sashmo stopped to contemplate the entire situation when a small yellow light came from behind a tree and hovered right in front of his face. The light dimmed down. It was then that Sashmo could see that the yellow light was Lilianna.

"Hello again big guy," said Lilianna.

"You don't have to worry about us anymore fairy. The quest is off. Nothing to tell the Council," replied Sashmo.

"I wouldn't say I'm worried. That's a bit strong. More like concerned."

"What would cause you to be concerned about us?"

"I am concerned about what is troubling you."

"Who said I was troubled?"

"Tough not to notice those big, sad eyes on a creature of your stature," replied Lilianna.

"Okay fine. You got me. It's just that I'm not the beast on Ellie's easel. I never will be."

A look of confusion flashed upon Lilianna's face.

"I want to save my friends. Be the hero for once. But I'm just Sashmo, the Unimpressive."

"It wasn't too long ago where I would have agreed with you on that," said Lilianna.

"Thanks for the kick while I'm down. You should hang out with Ellie more."

"You are yet to see it is all. When I first learned of you, I only heard one thing: grandson of the great Sagamo, son of Council member Sakemo, and not a thing like either one them," said Lilianna.

"That's exactly my point," said Sashmo.

"But the things I have witnessed from you over the last few days are anything but unimpressive. Impulsive, rebellious, quite silly at times, but not unimpressive," replied Lilianna.

"I'm alone in the snow. Completely lost in the Canadian wilderness. I'm defining unimpressive."

"But you aren't alone. For starters you have J.D. He has been your loyal companion from the first time you met. He would not leave your side even in the darkest of situations. He knows that you will

76

protect him from anything. You risked your quest, exposure, and the chance to save Abby just to rescue him. Sacrificing your own personal goals for a loved one is a characteristic of a hero."

"But," interrupted Sashmo

"But nothing," said Lilianna, "Did you not also once risk it all to save a helpless fairy?"

"I considered leaving you there. But you were trapped. We had to do something."

"Exactly! Does this not make you great? Does this not make you impressive? Is self-sacrifice not a worthy trait? Great power means great responsibility. Especially when it concerns the ones you love or in the name of the weak."

Sashmo nodded his head. He understood the point Lilianna was making. He began looking inside himself. Reflecting on all his life's decisions. Maybe he did have the potential to be a worthy addition to the line of great sasquatches before him. Maybe his father was wrong about him. Perhaps he could do something more.

Lilianna continued, "Is that not exactly what a Council member should be? A selfless protector of all mythical creatures, big and small?"

"You have quite the way with words Lilianna."

"Perhaps. Or perhaps you are more than anyone thought you were. Except Ellie! He's always believed in you Sashmo. That friendship is not just part of you. It's engrained in your DNA. You must find him and complete your quest. It is important," Lilianna said with a sense of urgency.

Sashmo was confused despite the pep talk from Lilianna. Despite feeling that maybe he was better than he believed, the idea of important was not one of the things that had crossed his mind.

"Important?" Sashmo said quite befuddled. "Why important?"

"No time for that now. We will see each other again soon."

"But wait."

"Godspeed Sashmo," Lilianna said with hope. "And don't worry, it won't hurt."

At that very moment, a creature from a short distance in the background pulled out some sort of weapon. The creature lined Sashmo up in his sights and fired one perfectly aimed shot. A dart swirled through the air, landing center mass of Sashmo. Sashmo looked down, saw the dart and started to pull it out of his chest. His knees grew weak beneath his massive body. He began to stumble around like a baby Wendigo taking its first steps. After a short moment, Sashmo slowly collapsed to the ground with a loud thud. J.D. turned to catch a glimpse of the creature attempting to reload. J.D. planted his feet in the ground and sprung into the air, desperately flying away. J.D. sailed into the distance as the creature put his dart gun away. He looked down to a watch-like device on his wrist.

"Sir, we have the Sasquatch. The Loch Ness Monster wasn't here. I do not have a location on him."

"And the God's mistake?" A voice radioed back from the transmitter.

"I was spotted. He got away. Arrange transport."

Chapter Thirteen: Enter Sandman

Sashmo awakened to find himself lying on the ground of what appeared to be a jail cell. He began to scan his surroundings. His cell was not very large and greatly restricted his movement. He stood as close as he could to the laser bars that encased him and attempted to look around. There were various cages down a long, low lit hallway. Sashmo could barely see, but was able to make out what appeared to be a Centaur and a Drop Bear. As his eyes continued to examine the hall, he noticed a pair of bright, grey eyes staring at him from the cell directly across from his own.

"Hey. Hey, hey. Were you just dreaming over there?" spoke a voice as slow as it was mysterious.

The voice came from the mythical creature known as the Sandman. Besides his glowing grey eyes, the Sandman had gritty, almost translucent white skin. His hair was jet black, wild, and seemingly untamed. It almost had a life of its own. No one knew the age of the Sandman. He was believed to be timeless, operating on a fourth dimensional plane that has no laws of time. The only thing that was really known about him was that the grit and grime creatures get in their eyes when they awaken from sleeping is the left over residue of his dream sand.

"Hello, who are, where am I?" Sashmo said, still struggling to gather his wits about him.

"You were. You definitely were. Above a dove right? Big, beautiful, white. Crashing into the moon."

"How could you…"

"Yup, dove. Nailed it. What are you in for?" The Sandman questioned, cutting Sashmo off mid-sentence.

"Could be a number of things."

Sashmo was starting to gain his footing, feeling as if he was back to normal when the Sandman reached in the pocket of his black coat, and slung dust into Sashmo's face, knocking him unconscious again. A few moments later, Sashmo's eyes shot open. He shook his fur and sat up in a rush.

"What, huh? What happened?"

"Dove again?" laughed the Sandman.

"Wait, who are…"

Sand again splashed over Sashmo's face. His gigantic body crashed to the floor once more.

A beautiful white dove sailed throughout a crystal blue sky. Its wings spread wide, catching the air and carrying the dove peacefully. Out of nowhere, grey clouds rushed into the sky surrounding it. Lightning began to crack viciously. Thunder roared. The dove was thrown off course and spiraled out of control. The dove pulled up, racing higher and higher into the sky to escape the harsh strikes of the lightning. The dove flew as fast as it could, until out of nowhere, the moon appeared in its path. The dove tried desperately to stop or

81

change direction, to no avail. The graceful white dove crashed into the moon.

At the very moment the dove crashed, Sashmo again bolted awake.

"What is going on?"

"Sorry, sorry about the dust brother. But the dove? The dove again?"

"Yes, the dove, the dove. Who are you? What is going on?"

Sashmo grew surprisingly impatient.

"Pardon my manners. I, I am Ole Lukoje. The Sandman. Master of dreams. Or used to be anyways."

"Sandman? I've heard of you. My father used to tell me stories. You and the boogeyman."

"Baba Yaga. My Sister. My opposite. Night and day. Yin and yang. Two sides, one coin. I brought the children visions of sugar plum fairies. She tormented their dreams. It's no surprise your father told you stories of her. He would have had the best ones. Helped put her away, me too, sort of," the Sandman reflected, with an ominous tone about him.

Sashmo was confused. His father's tales were always just those, tales. He never believed these stories were anything more than fairy tales, as ironic as that may have been.

"I had no idea," he said.

"When your grandfather passed, your father and the Hydra radically changed the path of the Council. The purpose of the Council was to unite and live peacefully with humans. Your grandfather's death changed everything. The humans could no longer be trusted. No contact with humans whatsoever. My sister couldn't change her ways, and as long as she sought to scare children, I had to be there to help. We were both put under tight surveillance. Neither of us stopped. We broke the new code," the sadness in the Sandman's heart could be heard in his voice.

Sashmo understood. "Never seen, never bother," he mumbled under his breath.

"Exactly! Exactly! Your father and the Hydra changed the course of history at the first and only special session of the Council. Let me show you."

The Sandman again reached into his packet, grabbed a patch of sand, and tossed it into Sashmo's face.

Fruit trees were present all over a picturesque landscape. This was the Island of Apples, Avalon. The mythical island was once an important part of Arthurian legend until his betrayal of Sagamo.

It was a rare place where vegetation outnumbered the fields. Exotic animals of all kind wondered about and a majestic castle sat, cradled by and hidden amongst the vast forest. Inside the castle, a great room housed a large table. Seated at the head of that table was Sakeamo, Sashmo's father, alongside a young Hydra. Around the table sat various leaders from other species of creature.

"We have called you all here today because there has been a disturbance in the rules that govern our society. As we have all become painfully aware, humans have broken the long standing truce that we have lived by," spoke Alpha, the dominant head of the Hydra.

Beta, the second of the Hydra's heads continued, "Therefore, we as mythical creatures agreed to end all contact with those savages."

"It has come to our attention," said Delta, the third head, "that the brother and sister duo of Ole Lukoje and Baba Yaga have not abided by our new code. We are putting this to a vote. Remember, this will set the precedent for the future of us all."

"This will be the proof of our commitment to the agreement we all made," added Gamma.

"Please, for the sake of the Council, make your voices heard," concluded Epsilon, the last of the Hydra's heads.

Hand by hand began to rise around the table. Sakeamo looked around as all the hands continued to rise. Disgust filled his soul.

"Wait!" screamed Sakeamo. "Do you all realize that by condemning these two that you are giving up your freedoms? Giving up your rights? I agree we must be cautious when it comes to the humans, but the line has to be drawn somewhere. We must still be able to maintain our lifestyles, our customs, and our ways. This may have no bearing to some of you. For others of you interacting with humans is how you survive."

A few hands begin dropping, slowly, taking to heart the words of the great Sasquatch.

"This coming from you Sakeamo, whose father was taken from you by those very monsters?" questioned Alpha.

Sakeamo knew the truth. His head dipped slowly. The weight of his father's death weighed on his heart. He wanted to do the right thing but at this moment he felt lost.

"A final show of hands," said Epsilon.

Again the hands began to rise, all of them.

Delta began to speak, "Then it is settled. Let the record show that meddling with humans will not be tolerated. In any circumstance."

"Hugin and Munin, fly to all the tribes and spread the word," said Beta.

"Never seen, never bother," proclaimed Gamma.

The congregation echoed, "Never seen, never bother."

As the other leaders left the hall, Sakeamo and the Hydra were all that were left.

"I don't think you truly realize what happened here today," Sakeamo said with a sense of defeat filling his voice.

"If we try to coexist with the humans again, history will repeat itself; it is only a matter of time. You weren't there that day with us and your father. You didn't see inside the soul of these humans the way we did. Think of your son. Do you want Sashmo growing up without a father?" asked Alpha.

"Of course not," responded Sakeamo, "I love Sashmo. However, I also want him to live in a world where he can choose his own path. If that means staying grounded here on Earth, or flying to the moon. Living amongst humans or not, then so be it. After today, he will never have that chance."

"It may not be an option," Gamma said, with a sense of understanding, "but are you willing to risk his safety for that chance?"

"Despite what happened to my father, I still have faith in the good of humans. What creature is not without its flaws, or its ability to redeem itself? But I realize I cannot create a society and then not live by the rules that have been voted upon. I shall live and raise Sashmo by the code."

"Excellent," concluded Alpha.

Sashmo again darted awake from his dream. Once again he was groggy, trying to find his footing. As he gathered his bearings, he was weighed down by emotional distress.

"I, I had no idea," said Sashmo, looking apologetically across the cells to the Sandman. "My father never told me that story. He always just said to run from humans. He recited it to me every night. Never seen, never bother! I had to recite it back to him."

"Well now you know," responded the Sandman. "What are you going to do now?"

As Sashmo was about to respond, a voice rang out from down the hall. "Sasquatch, awaken and place your arms outside the cell."

"Wait, Sandman, my father talked about me flying to the moon. You kept making me see the Dove, what does it mean?"

"You're the dove Sashmo, only you can bring peace to land. Don't crash."

The Sandman slid back into the darkness of his cell as the creature who called for Sashmo arrived in front of his cell. Sashmo placed his arms through the bars of the cell and the creature secured a set of cuffs around his wrists. Once the cuffs were tightly clasped, a beam shot up and encircled Sashmo's neck. A second beam shot downward to his feet and clasped around both ankles. The bars from the cell then went faint.

"Is all of this necessary?" Sashmo asked inquisitively, looking at his chains.

"We take no matters lightly. They are ready to see you now."

Chapter Fourteen: The P.E.T.

Sashmo entered into a dimly lit room. In front of him was a single desk and chair. He was ordered to sit and wait. Sashmo took his place at the table and a giant light ignited and began to shine aggressively into his face, throwing off his vision and making him rather uncomfortable. A door opened on the other side of the room and a strange silhouette came walking in. Sashmo could soon see that this creature has not one, but two heads. The two heads were strikingly similar to each other in appearance. Two necks came from a common focal point and positioned each head above either shoulder. They had large, elongated skulls and a deep, but shining green texture to them. Their eyes were glowing purple behind empty black voids. The creature waddled forth and took a seat at the table before Sashmo.

"A Council member. I must say Agent Tom, this is a unique opportunity indeed," said the first head, Agent Drozorkmog.

"I have to agree Droz, not every day that we get a creature up in here like this," continued the second head, Agent Tom.

Agent Drozorkmog continued, "Do you know who or what we are Sasquatch?"

"Droz and Tom," answered Sashmo, he had learned a few things from his father. "Heads of the Policing Extra Terrestrials. A third party policing unit brought to Earth under contract by the Council. Making sure we follow the code."

"Well it appears you are smarter than you may appear. Do you know why you are here?" asked Droz.

"Couple of guesses," joked Sashmo.

"Try one out," urged Tom, leaning in close to listen, "see how it fits."

"We got chased by hunters, J.D. destroyed a village, I exposed myself to save him. How'd I do? I miss any?"

"Exposed yourself! Never seen, never bother! I would think a creature of your lineage would understand the consequences of these actions," said Droz.

"I was trying to save a friend! Creatures like you probably wouldn't understand," Sashmo said, wondering in his heart just where poor J.D. might be.

"A friend wouldn't have gotten another friend into such a tight spot," Tom said.

"It was an accident. J.D. didn't know what he was doing."

Droz spoke up loudly, "And do you know what an accident like that costs?"

"What's the Canadian currency again?" Sashmo joked.

"No time for jokes Sasquatch, you know Canadians don't have currency, they trade in fur," Tom responded, looking at Agent Drozorkmog for confirmation.

Drozorkmog shook his head, obviously frustrated with his partner's response.

"The point is Sasquatch, your little stunt informed hundreds of humans of our existence putting all of our lives in danger," said Droz.

"Yeah. Well I'd do it again for J.D. or any other creature. It's what's right," Sashmo said proudly and with a slightest hint of arrogance not seen in him before.

"Speaking of this J.D.," Tom countered, "Where are he and the monster?"

Sashmo again wondered where poor J.D. could be. On top of that, this was the first time he'd had a chance to wonder about Ellie. "Was he ok? Had he gotten himself into trouble?" Sashmo thought. "No idea," Sashmo offered in feedback to the aliens.

"Your file says that you and Elliot 'Ellie' Ness are the closest of friends," Droz continued to question Sashmo. "That you live with him at the Loch. How do you not know where he and your pet are?"

Sashmo didn't hesitate, "I wouldn't give them up even if I did know."

"Things would be, let's just say, easier if you did," Tom said with a sense of intimidation.

"Your Councilship doesn't protect you here Sasquatch. The more you help us, the more we can help you," said Droz.

Sashmo reflected back on the past several days. Only a few weeks ago he was enjoying the lazy, unfettered life of living with Ellie at the Loch. He had no cares, no ambitions, and no path. He was perfectly content to stew away in the cave during the day, longing for Abby, but doing nothing about it. Hanging out by the water with J.D.

and Ellie at night, looking at the stars, it was a good if unfulfilled life. He was safe there. They were all content. Then after his father passed, and he had to take over at the Council everything started to change. He'd resisted it every step of the way, but slowly had grown into something more than he was. Something he could be proud of.

"A few days ago I might have given you everything that you wanted," Sashmo reflected, "but I've learned that just because something is, doesn't mean it is right."

Agent Drozorkmog was disappointed. He had hoped Sashmo would give in easier than that. "Wrong answer Sasquatch. Prepare the device."

"Awe man, we ain't got to do the boy like that," protested Agent Tom.

"I'm sorry," Sashmo said with a bit of hesitation, "Do me like what?"

Agent Drozorkmog and Agent Tom's body stood. They turned and began to walk out of the room. As they do Sashmo's chains lit back up again. He looked around, trying to figure out some sort of plan but he was trapped and there was nowhere to go. The creature that brought him to this room returns.

"This way," he barked as Sashmo stood, unsure what was to happen next.

Chapter Fifteen: Never Troll Quest

Ellie sat alone with his back against a tree as a light rain crept out of the sky and splashed against his scales. It felt nice for him to get refreshed, though the Canadian rain was much cooler than he was used to.

He held a small piece of wood in his hand. Using his rather sharp claws, he slowly whittled away at the tiny piece of tree. His art skills had to stay in practice after all. As he continued to whittle, he pulled his head back to observe and acknowledge his work. He had created a miniature Sashmo, down to the very last detail. "He'll be back," Ellie thought to himself. Since they met each other many moons ago, this was, as Ellie thought, the first fight the two of them had ever had.

"He probably thinks I'm just sooooo sad, sitting around crying," Ellie said aloud to himself as he wiped away a tear. "I'm not crying, it's just this rain."

A sudden noise disturbed his thought. He jumped to his feet, hoping to see Sashmo's colossal body emerging from the edge of the tree line. It was just a squirrel. His head dropped. Ellie continued to think about Sashmo. They had been inseparable. He contemplated all the other great duos of history. Tom Sawyer and Huck Finn. Pilgrims and Indians. Scrooge McDuck and his money bin. Hulk Hogan and the Macho Man. Ellie's imagination and thoughts started to get away from him. All of a sudden, as if blissful intervention, it came to him.

"Why didn't I think of this," he yelled to himself. "I'll just Gooblin him."

Goblin's are known for three very distinctive things: the grotesque warts that cover their skin, their less than amenable demeanor, and their widespread ability to track anything. For years, Goblins had been known as the greatest trackers in the mythical creature world. If anyone or anything needed to be found, creatures could Gooblin them (as it was referred to) for a small price. In recent times they had faced a little bit of competition from their arch-nemesis the Trolls, whose Troll Questing was not quite as effective, but required creatures to reach less into their pockets.

Ellie set out to find the closest Goblin clan to acquire their services in finding Sashmo. He eventually made his was to Goblin Bay, Canada. "Not a very inconspicuous name," he thought to himself. He noticed a nearby arching bridge in the distance and headed that way, knowing that Goblins enjoy themselves a good bridge to live under. As he got closer to the bridge, he noticed it was very rundown and the vegetation around it had overrun the area almost entirely.

"Hello?" he called out. "Hey goblins, you there?"

"Who goes there?" A loud, deep, echoing voice rumbled in response.

"I'm Ellie, better known as the Loch Ness Monster. Don't let the name fool you, I'm no monster, quite caring and affectionate actually. I'm here to Gooblin my friend."

"How do you know we are Goblins and not those rotten trolls?"

"I figured even trolls had too much pride to live in Goblin Bay."

"And why don't you find this friend of yours on your own? Do they not want to be found?"

"If it's going to be trouble, perhaps I could just Troll Quest him."

A petite and unpleasant humanoid creature standing just over 3 feet tall emerged from behind the brush. He had a thick body topped with an oversized and hairless head. Its face was covered with the well-known warts. It had massive ears and unblinking red eyes.

"Troll Quest is for the weak of heart," said the creature. "Impish is my name, Gooblining is my game. I suppose I can help you out. Now this friend of yours…"

Impish pulled out a pair of glasses from the pocket of his tattered pants and a notepad and pen from his back pocket.

"What does he look like?"

"He's a Sasquatch. Big, brown, hairy body. Big, brown, hairy head. Big, brown, hairy feet. Big, brown, and hairy. Yeah. Pretty stereotypical Sasquatch. No defining features or characteristics."

94

Impish sketched on his pad. He stopped for a moment and discerned his work. Ellie appreciated his artistic integrity. Impish began to frantically erase. Then draw once more. He repeated this process a few more times. Finally, he stopped and gestured his head in approval. He turned the drawing towards Ellie.

"Here, like this?"

Ellie looked at the picture. He changed his mind about that artistic integrity thought. It looked nothing like Sashmo. It didn't matter. "How many Sasquatches could possibly be lost out there?" he thought. Sashmo is the only one Ellie had ever known. He doesn't even know if there are anymore or not.

"Exactly," answered Ellie.

"How long has it been since you last saw this Sasquatch?"

Ellie was not sure as he was not great with time. He looked up at pointed towards the sky.

"The sun was about a half-a-click that way," he said.

"Not bad, I think we can handle this for you."

"We?"

"I'm not as spry as I once was, so I have a little assistance from the best kind of Goblin to do your tracking. The Hobgoblin. Henry!" Impish yelled. "Henry, get up here!"

There was no answer. Impish pulled back some brush to reveal what appeared to be a manhole cover. He began jumping up and down on it, yelling.

"Henry! I said get up here! We have a job!"

95

Impish strolled back over towards Ellie. The manhole began to move. Slowly, a younger, shaggier version of Impish protrudes out of it.

"Dude, Alright, alright man. I'm awake. I was playing a wicked game of Fortnite."

"I'd say that garbage is turning your brain to slush if it wasn't that way already. The monster here needs help finding his friend. You're doing it."

"Really dad? That's not cool man."

Impish grew increasingly irritated with Henry. He left no further room for discussion.

"The Hobgoblin here is going to be assisting you today. Don't let his slacker demeanor fool you, he really is the best."

"Awesome. Oh, and by any chance, do you guys find other things? Inanimate objects perhaps?" asked Ellie. "Hypothetically speaking, if someone was looking for a very specific set of VHS cassette tapes?"

Impish and Henry looked at each other and then turned their attention back at Ellie. The confusion on their faces read loud and clear to Ellie.

"No? That's a no. I got it."

Henry casted a final look of disgust at his father. His father in turn gave him one more look of "don't mess this up." Impish hands him the description of Sashmo. Henry walked up to Ellie.

"I last saw him heading," Ellie looks around, not sure which was his which, "let's say he was heading West."

"This should be fun. Alright bro, let's get it over with."

Chapter Sixteen: The Hobgoblin's Debt

Henry the Hobgoblin led Ellie deep into the Canadian wilderness.

"It's the only way we can travel with you around," said Henry.

Ellie understood and followed the Hobgoblin. He gave his blind faith that the hideous creature he trailed into the dim and creepy woods would ultimately lead him to reunite with Sashmo and back to the quest. Every so often, Henry lifted his nose into the air, sniffed around, and either continued his path or altered their route ever so slightly.

"I can see why you hate your job. If I had to sniff the downwind of a Sasquatch all day I'd be disgusted too," joked Ellie, trying to lighten the mood.

"Yeah bro, you have no idea. So how'd you lose this fella anyways? What was his name? Sashagawea? Sassafrass?"

"Close. Sashmo. We had a little falling out over a differing of ideas."

"Differing?"

"Yeah, that's a word."

"Sashmo huh? Like the newest Council Member? One of those ravens, the talkative one, Munin? Hugin? I don't know. They delivered us the news."

"Munin, that's the talkative one. But yes, that same Sashmo. We were on a quest."

Henry's ears perked up. Talk of a quest actually gained his interest in the conversation.

"Quest you say? You guys like trying to head to the moon or something? Apollo," laughed Henry.

"There's this oil drilling thing going down in Alaska," Ellie said, "We have to get there to stop it."

"Dude, that's the humans bro. Never seen, never bother," Henry responded.

Ellie seemed surprised that a Hobgoblin like Henry would care at all about the rules of the Council.

"That's why it was a secret quest. You see, where they are drilling is the home of the Yeti. My buddy just happens to be in love with one, Abby. So, it's kind of important."

"Now that you mention it, I think I did hear about that. Those dang ravens again. Didn't the Council rule not to do anything about all that?"

"Exactly, so it's up to us. We're going to stop them."

"Never seen, never bother bro."

Ellie went silent for a moment. Hearing an unscrupulous character like the Hobgoblin reflect on what they were doing caused him to second guess the entire quest for a moment. Ellie thought it may be crazy. "It doesn't even matter though", he thought to himself, "not unless we find Sashmo in time." Ellie retreated into his thoughts.

The Hobgoblin opened up the conversation yet again.

"So Dude, what exactly is that plan? We find the Sasquatch, you two get to the drilling. What are you going to do?"

Ellie contemplated the question. Usually he was full of ideas but this time he had no answer.

"No clue, I just know we have to hurry."

Henry suddenly stopped in his tracks. He put his nose to the ground and took a couple of huge sniffs. He shook his head. He then stood back to his feet. His nose cascaded around the air. As he sniffed harder, a disgusted look overtook his face.

"What kind of awful creature is making a smell like that?" asked Henry.

He pulled his nose out of the air as the slight bit of sun that hit them through the tree line was suddenly blocked out. A large, winged creature descended from the tree line like an angel down from Heaven. The glare around the creature prevented Henry from being able to see it. Ellie knew that silhouette from anywhere.

"J.D! What are you doing here?' screamed Ellie.

"And I thought Goblins were ugly. You know this monstrosity?"

"Henry, meet J.D., the Jersey Devil. He's Sashmo's pet. We must be close." Ellie was getting excited. "Where's Sash at buddy?"

J.D. ogled at Ellie. Ellie stared back. It's at this moment Ellie realized J.D. has no way to communicate with him. Ellie pulled out the Sashmo creature he had fashioned earlier. He handed it to J.D.

"Here boy," he says to J.D. "Show me using this."

J.D. circled around it. He investigated the wood carving of his owner Sashmo then suddenly leaned over and slurped it up into his mouth.

"He was eaten by a large, distasteful creature?" guessed Ellie.

J.D. looks frustrated at Ellie. He shook his head "no". He put the figure down again. Circled around it some more and then sucks it up again.

"He was trampled by a herd of dinosaurs?"

J.D. again shook his again. Ellie gave a few more fruitless answers.

"He was made King of the Orangutans? Was swept away by a slew of pixies? Jabbed his eye on a branch and went to the Lochtomitrist?"

The guessing continued as hours passed and Ellie proved to be quite incapable of playing a game of charades. As the time passed, they became less and less enthusiastic about trying to communicate anymore. Henry was also growing increasingly annoyed with the situation.

"Dude," chimed in Henry, "What if like, Sashnook got abducted by some aliens and they beamed him to Pluto. Which is totally a planet by the way."

J.D. began jumping up and down. He ran in circles, visibly excited, pointing his nose at Henry. Ellie was confused.

"Wait," Ellie said, "that's it?"

J.D. bounded again, nodding his head up and down.

"I can't believe Sashmo is on Pluto! Where are we going to find space suits at this hour?" Ellie said, shaking his head.

J.D. hung his head. He was embarrassed of Ellie. He looked back at Ellie as if to ask "are you serious?"

"Oh of course. Aliens! That means the P.E.T. must have him. That's not good."

"Well Bro," Henry said with a sense of relief in his voice, "looks like this is where I roll out. I don't mess with the P.E.T. dude."

"Yeah sure. I get it. Thanks for your help though Henry. You're not so bad for a Hobgoblin."

Ellie waved goodbye to Henry and wobbled himself onto J.D.'s back. J.D. expanded his wings and began to fly, struggling a bit with Ellie on his back.

"What?" Ellie said in disappointment, "I've been putting on a winter coat."

J.D. let out a sigh. He commenced to flap his wings harder and eventually he and Ellie lifted off the ground and flew away just over the tree line. Henry looked on, watching them leave his sight. Once out of distance Henry pulled out his phone and made a call.

"Yo J-Dawg! This is your boy the Hobgoblin. I need to speak with Mr. Williams," Henry said.

"Fa one, da boss is busy. Secondly, if you call me a dog again," responded Jacob, the werewolf and Williams' right hand goon.

"Okay, okay. I just have some information you might be interested in. For a price."

"This better be good... okay... who?... when?... That is good information. I'll talk to da boss and get back to you."

Both parties hung up the phone. Jacob put his phone in his pocket and ran to find Williams. In the distance, Lilianna was hovering. She had been following Ellie, ensuring that the quest went as planned. This new information concerned her greatly. She had an idea to help. Ellie would be fine without her. She flew off in a hurry.

Williams was walking with two other men out in the Alaskan wilderness. They were being followed and recorded by two reporters doing a segment on the oil drilling expedition. All three men were in heavy coats embroidered with "Fenris Petroleum." As Williams speaks with the reporters, pointing at this and that, Jacob spots them and catches up in a hurry.

"Hey boss. Got something for you," said Jacob.

"Go ahead," answered Williams.

"Nah, nah. Like alone."

"Very well. It seems as though the footage will have to do for you gentlemen. Just remember that in two days at dusk we will be holding the ribbon cutting ceremony for the project. Fenris hopes you all can attend."

Williams and Jacob trudged through the snow until they were out of hearing distance of the other men and the reporters.

"What is the problem Jacob?" asked Williams.

"You remember that Hobgoblin kid?" asked Jacob in return.

"Henry? Yes. Owes us quite a bit of money doesn't he?"

"Yeah that one. He called to clean his slate."

"Did he rob a leprechaun's pot of gold?" asked Williams.

"No. He didn't have any dough. He offered us info."

"Go on," pressed Williams.

"A-lleg-edly, there are some Sasquatch and a sea serpent, on their way here. They plan to stop the "humans" from drilling."

"A Sasquatch… and a sea serpent…? That's a peculiar duo. What in Valhalla for?"

"Looks like the Sasquatch has the hots for one of the Yeti around here. And he is a Council member."

"Council? I thought you said the Hydra declared no one was to stop us? No matter. We cannot allow the Hydra to get wind of any of this. How long until they arrive?"

"Don't know. The Sasquatch got captured by the P.E.T.s. But the serpent is trying to free him. Like nowish. Want me and the pack to take care of them?"

The thought of being able to go out and hunt down a sea serpent started to make Jacob's mouth salivate. Even in human form, his tongue started to hang out and his eyes changed color from green to a bright red.

"Put your tongue away. The P.E.T.s could ruin everything. We must handle this internally before they investigate further," replied Williams.

"Right. Good thinking boss."

"Get me the Yeti's name."

Chapter Seventeen: Prison Break

A dark room was modestly lit from the various advanced and shining technological gadgets that operated throughout the room. Agent Drozorkmog and Tom were sitting at a table. Their two heads leaning as far away from each other as possible. They played through several hands of some type of alien card game when things started to heat up between them.

"It's about that time my brother," Tom announced with a bravado to his voice, "I'm going all in right here."

Tom pushed his stack of chips to the middle of the table. He moved his head in assurance.

"You're bluffing," Droz replied, "the foot you control is twitching."

"If you are so sure why don't you call and let me get them chips."

"Your foot always twitches when you're bluffing."

Tom's face grew in despair. He knew he'd been called. Droz began to slide his chips towards the middle of the table when a Lieutenant burst through the door. He was so anxious that he bumped into the table, knocking the chips over and the cards out of Tom's grasp, revealing his losing hand.

"Forfeit, interference, erroneous, the hand cannot stand," Tom yelled with excitement.

"What is it Lieutenant?" Droz questioned in pure frustration.

"We have a situation sirs," the Lieutenant answered, "We have a creature outside."

"Man I was just about to win this hand," quipped Tom, "Can't you just zap it or something."

"I don't believe 'zapping it or something' would be protocol," Droz said shaking his head.

"Sirs, it's the Loch Ness Monster and what I can only guess to be one of Satan's minions outside."

Droz and Tom looked at each other in confusion. They jumped their body up and ran over to the window to see if the Lieutenant was not mistaken. When they got to the window they could see them. Ellie, sat on top of J.D. like a Roman riding a horse into battle. J.D. struggled to keep them both aloft.

"Hello!" Ellie called out, "Housekeeping! Anybody home?"

Droz opened the window.

"We're very happy you could be here Elliot."

"And I'm, I guess glad to be here?"

"Ellie, we're going to need you to step up off the beast," Tom commanded, "Come aboard the ship, your boy is waiting for you."

"So you do have him?" Ellie reached and rubbed J.D.'s head. "Good boy, you found him didn't you boy."

J.D. was happy and full of pride for a job well done. Ellie turned his attention back to Agent Droz and Tom. "I'm actually going to need you to release the Sasquatch."

Tom laughed hysterically. Droz did not find Ellie's demeanor or banter amusing in the slightest.

"Elliot, we both know that isn't going to happen, just come aboard, we can talk," Droz was getting more annoyed by the minute.

"No really guys," Ellie called out again, "I'm going to need you to release the Sasquatch." Ellie leaned over to whisper into J.D.'s ear. "Don't worry boy, I've got this. Well maybe. If not, get ready to fly your ugly tail off."

"C'mon brother," Tom too was growing more frustrated, "Don't make us get all medieval on you."

Droz was over the fun and games. He used his hand to press the infamous red button. Instantly the alarm raged throughout the ship. The red emergency lights flashed and all the crew scurried around to take their battle formations in preparation for an assault on Ellie and J.D. Droz wasn't playing games. The bottom of the spaceship began to open up a hatch to release retrieval drones. Ellie panicked. He decided to stall by asking the same request, but much slower. "This is a great idea," he thought to himself. "I said," adding ten extra syllables to every word, "Re-lease the Sas…"

At the very moment Ellie began to speak the last syllable the water beneath them and the spaceship began to quiver. The quiver became increasingly intense as a thunderous noise began to grow louder.

"What is that?" Droz questioned Tom.

Tom did not know. He had his head buried in Droz's shoulder and was shaking as much as the water. Soon a whirlpool opened up within the water and out of it emerged the Kraken. Kraken's head burst out into the air. He looked around to gather his surroundings when he spotted Ellie.

"Oh hey, it's you again," Kraken said to Ellie, "What's going on cousin?"

"We'll catch up in a minute," Ellie was confused but instantly had a plan. "You remember my friend Sashmo?"

"Yeah, yeah, sure. Sasquatch. Questing for love."

"He's in the spaceship there. We need him out."

Kraken turned and looked at the spaceship. Tom still had his head deep into Droz's shoulder. Kraken then turned back to Ellie.

"He's in, you want him out? Got it."

Kraken turned back around to face the ship. By this time several of the retrieval drones had been armed and made their way out of the opening in the bottom of the ship. They took turns running attack formations at the Kraken. In one fail swoop, Kraken lifted his numerous tentacles from beneath the ocean surface and slapped them all out of the sky.

Kraken then turned his attention to the spaceship itself. He surrounded it with even more tentacles and began to squeeze. The metallic covering of the ship began to give and crack. The Kraken shook the spaceship all around the sky. The crew of the ship slammed around the halls, bouncing off the walls and ceilings alike. Prisoners rattled around their cells.

"I need one Sasquatch please," Kraken laughed. "Darn vending machines never give you what you want."

By this time Droz and Tom were also bouncing all around the card room. The chips and cards were flung all about. Their heads bounced off of each other. Tom was ready to relent.

"Yeah, sure," Tom said as they bounded off the control board. "One Sasquatch coming right up."

"No!" Droz answered defiantly, "We're actually going to need you all to surrender."

Kraken shook a few times harder then stopped for a moment.

"What's that you say? I seem to have water in my ears still."

Kraken shook his head violently as water sprayed out of both ears. He cracked his neck and placed his giant eye up to the window to the room Droz and Tom were in. "Yeah, can you repeat that?"

"Psych!" Tom answered. Droz's head was drooping to the side; he had been knocked out during the last couple of shakes. "He's playing dog. We'll get you the Sasquatch if you can promise me not to do that anymore."

"Yeah sure," answered Kraken, "I think we can make that deal."

Tom radioed in the command. A few moments passed before Sashmo emerged around the corner. Sashmo was filled with excitement and confusion. "Why was the Kraken here," he wondered.

110

It did not matter. He knew he was free. He walked over to the window. Kraken backed away and offered a tentacle. Sashmo climbed through a hole and out onto the outstretched appendage of the Kraken. It's there he saw J.D. and Ellie.

"Ellie!" Sashmo screamed.

"We got you big guy, it was all part of the plan," said Ellie.

Kraken wrapped a few more tentacles around the ship and placed it over his head.

"It's a little hat," he said, "it's funny."

He then started to pull back as if he was going to frisbee toss it hundreds of miles away before Sashmo interrupted.

"Kraken! Thanks a lot man," Sashmo spoke with the glee of a cubsquatch, "but before you dispose of that ship. I need one more favor."

"Yeah, yeah, sure Sashmo."

Sashmo peered into the window, looking for Droz and Tom.

"Agent Drozorkmog, Agent Tom, I need you to let the Sandman go as well. He doesn't deserve to be here."

Tom came forward, Droz was still out cold. "You're pushing your luck bro, but it doesn't appear we have any options here now do we?"

"Not this time," Sashmo answered confidently.

Agent Tom knew he had no other choice at this time. He again radioed to the crew to have the Sandman released. The crew members appear shortly with the Sandman in tow. They released him from his constraints and he exited the window onto another tentacle of the Kraken.

"I can't thank you enough Sashmo. I have been on that ship for what feels like an eternity. I owe you one." The Sandman reached out to shake hands and Sashmo returns the favor.

"I don't exactly know the etiquette for owing people, but I'd like to cash that in right now if I can." Sashmo stepped away from earshot of Ellie and whispers in the Sandman's ear. The Sandman giggled and nodded his head.

"Done. We're square."

"Sure are. Take care of those children."

"You too. Friendly dreams!"

The Sandman spun in a few circles and in a cloud of dust disappeared.

"Yeah so, can I fling this ship now?" asked the Kraken.

"Yeah, but be gentle," answered Sashmo.

The Kraken again pulled back, cracked his neck for good measure, and slung the P.E.T.'s ship. It vanished quickly into the distance.

Sashmo and Ellie looked at each other. They both casually shrugged, accepting each's others gesture as an apology and hugged it out.

"I can't believe you guys came back for me," Sashmo claimed.

"Of course we did big guy," Ellie responded.

J.D. jumped up and down and wagged his tail. Nothing more was needed to be said.

"We can worry about this mushy stuff later. We're running out of time for a quest aren't we?" Sashmo said with a pep in his step he had not had at the onset of the adventure.

"Exactly, a quest! But wait," Ellie turned to the Kraken, "thanks Krak, that was awesome."

"Yeah, yeah, no problem Ellie. No problem at all. Those aliens are always a bit hasty about things. I'm just glad you knew how to find me."

Ellie was confused, "How did a find you again?"

"Yeah, you know, all you have to do is say release the Kraken three times," the Kraken boasted proudly, placing a couple other tentacles on his hip.

"But I said release the sasq...yup, you are right. Release the Kraken three times."

"Well, I must be off," the Kraken swam the duo to the closest shoreline and placed them back on dry land.

"Thanks again," Ellie and Sashmo both called out. The Kraken quickly submerged himself back into the water with a monstrous splash and was gone.

"Okay Ellie, J.D., times wasting. We have to save Abby and the other Yeti; my father would want me to do this."

Sashmo continued to speak more confidently than Ellie had ever seen out of him before. A small grin came across his face.

"Alright Captain, this way," Ellie quipped.

"Actually, it's this way."

The two friends laughed and took off with a smiling J.D. flying just behind.

Chapter Eighteen: The Big Bad Wolf

The Yeti have resided in the frozen forest of Alaska's wilderness since the beginning. The ice-covered trees and landscape had provided the Yeti with the comfort of safety and anonymity even before the truce was broken and the mythical creatures had adopted the policy of never seen, never bother.

Abby sat on a snow-covered tree stump outside of the Yeti village. Her emotions overwhelmed her as she lamented about the inevitable Yeti migration. She once was strong and had great intentions of saving her kind; now everything seemed hopeless. There was nothing left to do but to move from the only home she had ever known, out into the unknown of the wilderness.

As she sat and sulked, a beautiful snow leopard approached from behind her. The leopard nestled her head against Abby, slightly startling her. Abby began to pet her affectionately.

"Hello Sheeba. I know how you feel. All we can do is just sit back and wait."

Sheeba snuggled even closer to Abby, offering what little comfort she could.

"We can just be endangered together," said Abby.

About that time Abby heard something coming towards her. She heard branches crashing and heavy breathing. Abby turned

115

towards the noise and out came a male yeti. It was Aboson, Abby's brother.

"Sis, come quickly. The migration has begun."

The two rushed back to the Yeti village, Sheeba close on their heels. They ran to their village, fully constructed of ice. There were small huts, a schoolhouse, a general store and a playground.

Aboson led the way. When they came into view, Abby stopped short of entering the village because the sight before her caused her to freeze. All the Yeti of the village, her friends, family and everyone she's ever known were outside their huts holding as much of their belongings that they could carry. Tears came to Abby's eyes.

"There's no time for that sis. We must go," said Aboson.

Abby followed Aboson back to their hut where their father, Solak stood.

"Do you have all you need for the journey Abby?" asked Solak.

"Yes father. What is the plan?" said Abby.

"We are going to head north and hope," responded Solak.

"We have no other choice," said Aboson.

Abby tried to stop more tears from falling.

"No! There has to be another way. We are being sent to the northern wilderness to start all over. Everything we have ever known is here," said Abby.

"Faith is a strong thing Abby. Sometimes you just have to trust in the Spirits and believe," said Solak.

"Father, this isn't a time for faith," said Abby.

"One must make time for it daughter," said Solak.

"Right now all I see is time to finish packing so that we can be run out of our home. Our home we have had for centuries," said Aboson angrily.

"Stop! Just stop. How can we be fighting at a time like this?" Abby asked.

Abby, began to cry again. She ran back into the woods. She was so overwhelmed that she did not pay attention to just how deep into the forest she ran. She got to the point where she could run no further. She found another log. Again she sat down and began to cry uncontrollably. After a few moments, Abby was startled by a sound in the near distance. It sounded like an animal whimpering. Abby followed the noise until she came upon a wolf caught in a bear trap.

"Hey little guy. It's going to be okay. I know it hurts," said Abby.

Abby used what strength she had left to pry open the trap from the wolf's leg.

"Are you okay?" asked Abby.

The wolf began to hobble away. Abby felt even more sadness in her heart witnessing the wolf suffer. The wolf suddenly stopped and turned back to look at Abby. Just as Abby began to feel a true sense of wonderment, she heard growls coming from behind her. She turned to see three other wolves staring her down like their next meal.

The wolf that Abby saved hobbled to her side and commenced to growl back, protecting the creature that just saved it. Two of the three wolves from the pack pounced on the injured wolf. With a hurt leg, it was no match for the two healthy wolves and was quickly beaten and thrown to the side. Abby turned to run but the third wolf was behind her. She was completely surrounded. Then Abby's fear turned to bewilderment as the leader of the wolf pack began to transform into a human. Williams stood in front of her.

"It is truly a shame that we are going to have to do this to you young lady," said Williams.

"Oh my, you're…"

"Indeed I am. And I am going to need you to come with me," said Williams.

Abby again tried to run away. She ran towards the two other members of the trio that have also turned into humans. She tried to fight them off but they eventually took her to ground and tied her up.

"I am truly sorry for this. But in my line of work, you leave nothing to chance," said Williams.

Williams walked away. Abby continued to struggle, as one of the men stuck her with a tranquilizing dart. Abby passed out and the two men drug her limp body through the snow, following Williams.

Several hours later, Abby woke up. She tried to orient herself but there is nothing but darkness to be seen. She managed to get to her knees and reached out. All she felt were cold steel bars and hopelessness. Innately she screamed out, "Let me out of here!"

A couple moments passed and the creaking of a large metal door opening is heard. The light coming in blinded Abby for a moment. Once her eyes adjusted, Williams could be seen standing in front of the cage.

"I'm happy you're awake. I trust your accommodations are well?" asked Williams.

"Lovely," replied Abby.

"I wanted to drop by and apologize again. I was perfectly happy simply letting you march to your demise with the rest of your species. You really do deserve to be with them," said Williams.

"You're insane, how dare you do this?" Abby said.

'How dare I? I believe Charles Darwin would ask 'How dare you'?"

"How does the Council not know what you are doing?" asked Abby.

"The Mythical Creatures Registration Act has its flaws."

"But all the Yeti…"

"Just another part of the circle of life. Your species falls to the bottom of the food chain, whereas mine goes straight to the top," said Williams.

"Straight to the top?" asked Abby.

"You cannot begin to comprehend the power of the moon and how much we crave it. Even more so during a full moon. Here is the prime location where we, the werewolves, can live under the moon year round. Our species will thrive, we will grow and prosper and soon not even that five-headed imbecile and all his merry men will be able to stop us from ruling the Earth. Thanks to his idiotic 'never seen, never bother' no know even knows you're here to help you. Except your boyfriend. Which will not be anything more than a minor hitch in our plan."

"My boyfriend?" asked Abby.

"The Sasquatch. And his friend, the Loch Ness Monster. It appears that they are on a mission to save you. Unfortunately for them and you, they have lost the element of surprise. I must go now. The moon is rising."

Williams walked out of the room, closing the door behind him. Abby was again in nothing but darkness.

Even with all of the information that Williams just divulged to her, Abby could only think of one thing he said. For the first time in a long thing she was able to utter a single word that bestowed hope back in her soul.

"Sashmo."

Chapter Nineteen: The Trail of Tears

A full moon slowly raised into the night sky. Sashmo, Ellie, and J.D. continued walking through the frozen wilderness of Canada, knowing they must be closing in on their final destination. For the first time during the journey there was no sense of dread and insurmountable odds. Instead there was a sense of excitement, duty, and of a coming accomplishment. Sashmo walked proudly, his chest out as he was flanked by his best and loyal two friends. Ellie, noticed Sashmo walking with a purpose. He winked at J.D. and slowly started to lag behind. As Sashmo got about 25 feet out in front of him, Ellie rolled a snowball up in his flippers and flung it at the back of Sashmo's head. J.D. instantly began pointing at Ellie as Sashmo turned around. Sashmo, shook the snow from his fur, laughed, and took off charging after Ellie. Ellie wasn't quick or nimble enough to get out of the way and was trampled into the snow by a rushing Sashmo. They toiled around a bit. J.D. bounced in excitement and finally they stood up.

"Since I'm done beating you up, back to questing then," laughed Ellie.

"Yes, I don't know how much time we have."

They continued their journey. Everything was going fine when they heard gunfire.

"Hunters," Sashmo said, "Stay close and stay small."

"Small? Like that's an option?" Ellie responded.

"You know what I mean," Sashmo said, "no time for mistakes now."

The trio continued moving forward, ducking and hiding behind each tree as they went. Soon the gunshots were but a faint echo in the background as they were finally out of danger. At this point Sashmo looked ahead and a big smile came across his face.

"Well will you look at that guys," Sashmo said as he pointed at a sign just outside the woods. A giant sign along their trail read, 'Welcome to Alaska.' Sashmo placed his arms around the shoulders of his pals as the moon continued its slow crawl towards the top of the sky.

A few hours down the road, Ellie spoke up. "We're close," he said.

"Are you sure?" Sashmo knew to question Ellie in such a situation.

"It's a hunch."

"One of your good hunches," Sashmo asked, "or one of the normal hunches."

"Hard to say."

"Ok, I'm going to look ahead," Sashmo responded. "You and J.D. just stay put, please."

Ellie knew that's what Sashmo wanted; but he also knew what was likely to happen.

"No promises," he said with a sly grin.

"No games Ellie. Stay here, keep your head down, and keep J.D. and yourself out of trouble."

Sashmo walked out from behind the tree and moved stealthily through the woods. He slowly came up on a clearing in the path and noticed figures moving in the distance. He positioned himself hidden from view to observe the oncoming movement. He glanced around the corner to take a look. His fur began to stand up on his arms and neck. His heart sunk and it felt like the wind was instantly knocked out of him as if he'd just taken a giant sucker punch to the gut. Thousands of Yeti were marching towards him down a hidden trail in the woods. They marched in uniform. Their heads hung in shame and sacks were thrown over their shoulders. Many pulled sleds behind them that were piled with supplies tethered together.

A tear formed slowly in the corner of Sashmo's right eye and slowly rolled own his check, streaking the hair on his face as it fell. Sashmo saw Abby's father, Solak, and her brother Aboson leading the march. He stepped out from his hiding place.

"Aboson," Sashmo called out.

"If it isn't Sashmo, the noble Councilmember," Aboson said as the two embraced in a hug of friendship. "You remember my father," Aboson gestured to Solak.

"Yes, at my father's resting ceremony. It's a pleasure sir."

"As to you Sashmo. If only it could be in better times," Solak spoke as he reached out to greet Sashmo.

"What's going on?" Sashmo asked. "Has the drilling already started?"

"The ribbon ceremony is tomorrow. We had to get out while we still could."

"Where are you heading?'

"We don't know."

Sashmo scanned the group. He noticed Abby was nowhere to be seen.

"Where's Abby?" he asked.

"We had an argument and she stormed off," said Solak.

"You didn't wait on her?" Sashmo said.

"Son, we are the leaders of this pack and we needed to lead. She is a big Yettete, she will find her way to us."

"Why are you here anyway?" Aboson asked.

Sashmo did not know why but he felt like something was wrong. Abby was stubborn but she would never let her people leave without her. His gut started to cramp.

"Well, I was, trying to save her."

"Save her from what son? There is nothing that can be done," said Solak sounding defeated.

"I don't believe that sir. There has to be something I can do."

"If you don't mind spending the rest of your life in a P.E.T. cell, of course there is. But the Council has spoken."

"You better just head on home Sashmo," Aboson offered as advice.

124

"With all due respect, I've already spent some time in a P.E.T. cell and I have no intensions on going back. But if this is Abby's world, then I have to save it."

"And what will you do?"

Sashmo thought for a second. They were right, he did not have a plan. But he or Ellie rarely had it all figured out. All he knew was that time was running out and he had to do something.

He looked Solak in the eye, "Something. I'll figure it out and make work."

Aboson laughed, "You sound just like Abby."

"She rubs off on you," Sashmo joked, "but now I have to go find her."

Sashmo turned to run back to Ellie and J.D. as Solak reached out and grabbed him firmly by the arm.

"Godspeed Sasquatch. If you manage to save our people, the Yeti will forever be in your debt."

Sashmo nodded to Solak, bid farewell to him and Aboson, and returned to Ellie and J.D. Behind him the Yeti continued their march into extinction. Sashmo scampered through the woods and eventually found his way back to where he left Ellie and J.D.

"Ellie? J.D.?" he called out.

They were nowhere to be found. Sashmo began to panic. Suddenly, he heard something coming from a portion of bushes. He approached the area where the sound was coming from slowly and peered his head around to take a look. There he saw Ellie lying on his back with J.D. jumping all over him, playing around.

"No, no, no. Stop J.D.," Ellie cackled. "That tickles."

"Seriously?" Sashmo said as he stepped around the bush.

"Okay," replied Ellie, "He's grown on me. You find anything ahead?"

"Well, you were right," Sashmo said in surprise, "We are really close. I saw the Yeti, all of them. Marching away from their homes. All of their belongings packed up with them. It was awful Ellie."

"So Abby knows we are here?"

"She wasn't with them. I have a bad feeling."

"That's odd right?"

"Really odd. She had a fight with her dad and brother, then ran off. They had to take the pack without her. She should have caught up with them by now."

"Ok, well here's the plan," Ellie said. Sashmo cut him off.

"Whoa there. I got his one. Abby's father mentioned the ribbon cutting ceremony was tomorrow. That's where I make my move."

"Perfect," Ellie was getting excited. He always loved when a plan came together. "We sabotage the whole thing so the drilling doesn't start. The land isn't destroyed. Abby and the Yeti keep their home."

"Something like that," responded Sashmo. "Except it isn't a 'we.' It's got to be 'I.' I have to do this."

"Say what?" Ellie was confused.

"This is my quest buddy. It's time for me to save the day."

Ellie smiled. He always knew his buddy could be a leader. It was not time to be sentimental however.

"Who are you?" he said, "And what have you don't with my pal?

"Just a big, dumb Sasquatch trying to save a Yeti."

Ellie started to sniffle. He couldn't keep it in.

"J.D. get a tissue," he said through the tears, "This is beautiful. What's the plan?"

Meanwhile, Williams and the rest of the werewolf pack were in the midst of final preparations. The Fenris Petroleum sign hung lavishly behind a podium upon the stage. Light stands were set up all around and amongst the chairs where the reporters in attendance will be sitting during the announcement. Jacob was issuing orders to the crew as Williams approached.

"When the setup is finished come find me. In the mean time I have some business to tend to."

"Yes sir boss," Jacob answered.

Williams walked around behind the stage to the storage container that was housing Abby. He entered the passcode into the key pad and slowly opened the door.

"Are you well dear?"

Abby was sobbing, "Leave me alone."

"You really should be more grateful my dear. You'll be seeing your Sasquatch soon enough."

"Don't hurt him," Abby cried, "You've done enough."

"I assure you I will not lay a hand on him. Perhaps a paw though," laughed Williams.

Abby did not understand. "This could all go another way," she said, "We could live on this land together."

"I'm afraid my mother never taught me how to share," Williams said with a sneer. "Get comfortable my dear, it's almost show time."

Williams laughed as he once again shut the door on Abby. The sun was in its slumber. The moon stood high above the press conference stage. The stage was complete. A giant red ribbon was pulled from one side to the other. The crowd was starting to fill into the seats. Reporters and cameramen surrounded the platform, all vying for position. Jacob came around the corner behind the curtain to find Williams.

"Boss, Boss. Everything is set up. We just got word the Bigfoot's coming."

"Excellent," Williams responded. "Get everyone into position. This should be fun."

"You sure this is the best plan boss? Maybe we just take the Bigfoot down in the woods?"

Jacob began salivating again at the idea of hunting Sashmo.

128

"If this Sasquatch thinks he is a hero, we are going to give him a proper hero's moment," Williams again began to laugh, "Then a proper hero's demise."

"Ah man, I never get to have any fun."

As Jacob runs back out to the front to give a few of the pack some final directions, Williams simply adjusted his tie, waiting.

Chapter Twenty: Show Time

Along the tree line, Sashmo sat on a tree stump roughly 200 feet from the stage. Ellie stood in front of him. He paced back and forth, frantically shaking and waving his hands into the air.

"Nope, non, nein, naamik, iie, dooda, nyet, and nullua," Ellie berated Sashmo.

Sashmo was impressed, "Did you just say no in all eight different languages you know?"

"Si," joked Ellie.

"How is it you know eight different languages again?"

"Yo quiero la biblioteca," answered Ellie.

"You just said 'you want the library'."

Ellie shook his head, "I never said I was fluent."

Sashmo laughed at Ellie. Even at a time like this Ellie knew how to make him giggle.

"None of that matters," Ellie said, "This is absolutely not the plan."

"It's the best one we have," Sashmo explained.

"Really," Ellie said visibly upset. "That's the best option you have? And you think my ideas are bad. If I only had my easel and had those Bob Ross tapes. Let me play it out for you. You sneak through the woods, coming upon the giant, multi-million-dollar press conference. There are hundreds of reporters gathered, excited to get coverage of this historic drilling expedition. Then, boom, you jump out of the woods, screaming to them about killing the Yeti. They don't hear anything you say because they all have dumbfounded looks on their faces or they are running away terrified with fear. Meanwhile those wonderful and cute Aliens we met earlier are just sitting around, playing whatever card game it is they play against themselves. When wouldn't you know it, the red phone, green alarm, or purple haze alerts them that the code is being violated. So they fly over to see what's going on. Before they get here though, the few humans that haven't ran away in fear are now hovering around you. They stare, still not caring about what you have to say because they can't believe that Big Foot really exists! Then, one of them gets a happy trigger finger and boom, you're filled with buckshot or worse. That doesn't kill you, cause look at the size of you. It does however take you off your feet and now they are trying to capture you. You get whisked away to be a center ring attraction at the circus or hang out with Kory the Gorilla at the San Diego Zoo. The Council can't protect you at this point because they are now scrambling to ensure the rest of the creatures are safe who WEREN'T IDIOTIC ENOUGH TO EXPOSE THEMSELVES AT A LIVE NEWS CONFERENCE!"

Ellie took a huge breath as he finished, keeled over a bit and started panting.

"Feel better?" Sashmo said with part grin, part reality setting in smirk.

"Much."

"Anything else?"

"No," Ellie answered, "I feel pretty good about it. Did it work?"

"Not a bit."

"Perfect. So how can I help?"

"You don't Ellie. I told you. I have to do this. If I end up in a cage in San Diego at least I'll know you and J.D. are safe."

"But," Ellie did not know what to say, "Sash…"

"Weren't you the one always telling me to Sasquatch-up?"

"Yeah but what a time for you to finally listen to me."

Sashmo smiled at his friend. "Just wish me luck and get J.D. out of here."

Ellie smiled back. He was worried about Sashmo, but proud of him.

"Good luck Sash."

J.D. was standing to the side. He was whimpering uncontrollably. His head hung and he slowly walked over to where Sashmo was standing. He snuggled his head into Sashmo's chest. Sashmo petted him like it could be the last time.

"Okay J.D. You have to go with Uncle Ellie. You listen to what he says now and take care of him. And no pillaging any villages. He'll feed you," Sashmo said.

Then he gave J.D. a giant sized hug. J.D.'s slobbering tongue ran across Sashmo's face.

"It's okay boy. I promise. Now go with Ellie."

132

"Be safe buddy," Ellie told Sashmo.

They looked at each other for a moment. Sashmo nodded his head and Ellie exchanged a nod in return. Ellie and J.D. scampered off into the woods as Sashmo turned and began walking closer to the tree line. Just off in the distance Ellie stopped and looked at J.D.

"I don't know about you buddy," smiled Ellie, "but I'm not going anywhere."

Sashmo worked his way slowly and quietly through the woods. He saw the lights of the press conference through the end of the tree line and knew that he was close. The full moon towered over the sky as Sashmo ducked behind a cluster of bushes just outside the clearing. Williams walked up onto the stage and stood before the podium. Sashmo listened in.

"This is momentous day. Fenris Petroleum is moving to the top of the world's oil food chain. Breaking ground today is but the first step in Fenris becoming the dominant oil company in the world."

Sashmo steadied his breath. His nerves began to take him over as he had to calm himself down.

"Okay Sash, here you are. 4,000 miles and the love of your life. It's time to be a hero." He stood up from his crouched position behind the bushes. His chest bowed up as the hair on the back of his neck rose. His eyes were filled with a look of determination that they had never been filled with before.

"As we move into the future," Williams continued, "Fenris will have a unique opportunity to both serve the people of the world while being a friend and protector of this beautiful Alaskan landscape…"

Sashmo has heard enough. He leaped from behind the bushes with all his might. His body sailed through the air, casting his silhouette in front of the moon. He flew so high it appeared as if he might almost crash into the moon itself, just like the dove from his dream. He remembered what the Sandman had told him. Don't crash. This was his moment. As he came down, his feet smashed onto the ground with a thunderous sound. He let out a monstrous scream as he banged his chest.

"Friend and protector? How can you call yourself that as you drill here with no regards for the lives you are destroying?"

Sashmo looked around. The crowd of people stared in awe at him. He resorted back to his and Ellie's tension breaking humor.

"I'm a Sasquatch. Yes, we exist. And talk." He returned to his message. "At this moment, thousands of Yeti are marching through the Alaskan countryside to their inevitable doom. A species as old as man itself, soon to be extinct because of what you are doing here today. We've lived for centuries with a code, 'never seen, never bother.' We've allowed humans to have free reign of this planet out of fear. My father would have wanted me to break that code to do what is right. That's why I stand before you today, to tell you there is no way I can allow you to drill here. Not now, not ever."

Williams stood upon the stage and began clapping. He walked to the edge and down the steps towards Sashmo.

"Quite a noble speech sasquatch," he said as he continued to clap.

Sashmo was confused. "What? How?" He looked around and noticed that no one had budged from their original positions. They all glared at him. They stood as smiles came across their faces as they too began to clap and encircle him. The clouds moved across the sky allowing the full light of the moon to shine.

"We've been expecting you Sasquatch," gleamed Williams. "Allow me to introduce myself. My name is Constantine Williams, Alpha of the Siberian Werewolf Pack. These are my brothers," Williams gestured to the crowd of people who now completely surrounded Sashmo.

"Werewolves? But how?"

"Being half-human gives you certain advantages in dealing with the Council. Even with five heads it's hard for your precious Hydra to keep an eye on all of us. Especially when he doesn't know we are out here. We've grown quite tired of hiding who we are. Exhausted with being an elite species on this planet and having to masquerade as a pitiful human. Here, with the moon above us, werewolves from all over can find a home, be proud of what they are. Soon we will be more powerful than the humans or Council could ever imagine."

"There are rules Williams," Sashmo said, "You can't do this."

"You are a fine one to talk about rules after that performance."

"I'm not murdering an entire species for self-satisfaction."

"Neither are we," said Williams. "We are simply taking the land we rightly deserve. The Yeti have every opportunity to survive if they manage and soon we will no longer have to hide from the humans, Council, or anything."

"So you plan to co-exist with the humans?"

"Who said anything about coexistence?"

Sashmo was feeling the pressure of the werewolves around him.

"I can't allow you to do this," Sashmo demanded.

"I think you will," Williams motioned to Jacob, who stood on the stage. "Jacob, the curtain please."

Jacob pulled aside the curtain that ran along the back of the stage. There sat a cage with Abby inside of it. Beside her cage were two other cages. One cage held Ellie and the other held J.D.

"Abby," Sashmo called out. He began to move towards her but the men surrounding him denied his advances.

"Yeah, hey to you Sashy," joked Ellie.

"Sashmo, you did come for me," Abby cried out for him.

"Of course I did," Sashmo responded.

Ellie took time to joke again, "Looks like another well executed plan buddy."

"I thought I told you and J.D. to go home."

"I'm going to assume you knew I wouldn't listen."

"I hate to interrupt this touching reunion," said Williams, "but we have more pressing matters to attend to."

"Which starts with you letting them go," Sashmo said boldly.

"I'll be happy to do so," Williams answered, "I'll let them go. You all leave and never return. We all go back to our business like none of this ever happened. Or, we destroy you all and I go back to my business anyway."

"I've ran from things my entire life Williams," Sashmo reflected, "I'm not running today."

"Oh but you should my dear boy. Look at the moon. So full tonight. Isn't it beautiful?"

Abby was scared.

"Just go Sashmo. We'll find a new home for the Yeti. We'll figure it out."

"No! This ends here," Sashmo said defiantly. "It's more than just saving the Yeti Abby. These dogs are violating everything the Council stands for. Everything my family helped build."

"Poor choice Big Foot. Take him boys."

"It's about time," said Jacob.

Williams stared at the moon and began to howl. Slowly, the men surrounding Sashmo all joined in, letting out screeching howls. Their muscles began to twitch and grow three times their normal size. Hair erupted from underneath their skin, covering their bodies. Their snouts protruded from their faces and their ears grew to points. Their teeth extend into razor sharp fangs as they salivated from their mouths.

"Hey Ellie, is there a plan B?" asked Sashmo.

Sashmo looked at the three cages on the stage. There's nothing he wouldn't do for those three. They were his family. He must protect them.

"I'd go with don't lose!"

Sashmo let out a ferocious roar of his own, drowning out the howls of the wolves. He pounded his chest as the werewolves moved in and engulfed him. Sashmo emerged from the pile. Werewolves flew through the air and hit the ground all around him. A werewolf leapt and bit Sashmo by the arm. He ripped him off with the other arm and threw him into a tree. Abby gasped as Sashmo continued to struggle.

"There's that Sasquatch blood!" Ellie yelled on in encouragement.

Sashmo reached out and grabbed another werewolf. Sashmo balled him up and rolled him like a bowling ball into another group of werewolves. They tumbled and fell to the ground as the wolf barreled through them.

"Strike!" Ellie said.

J.D. spit a fireball from his cage and hit one of the wolves on the back, setting his fur ablaze like the Eternal Flame of Hercules. Ellie signaled with approval. Two more werewolves jumped onto Sashmo's back. They dug their teeth into his massive shoulders. Sashmo reached back, grabbed them both and slammed them onto the ground in front of him.

"That's what I call a twofer," said Ellie.

Williams remained away from the fight grimacing as he watched his pack struggle with the Sasquatch. Jacob now joined in. He hit Sashmo with a series of blows, climbing all over Sashmo's weakening body and brought him down to one knee.

"Remember me from the Council Meeting Big Foot? I've been waiting to say hello again," smirked Jacob.

Abby clutched the bars of her cage. She pulled and strained with every muscle in her body to budge the bars but she failed. Jacob and Sashmo rolled around on the ground, exchanging blows. Jacob had control when Sashmo used a final surge of energy to snatch Jacob by the back of the neck and sling him into Ellie's cage. Ellie stuck his tail out of the cage and put a choke hold onto Jacob to keep him contained. He slapped him in the face with the tip of his tail and then released him. This was just in time for J.D. to send out another flame. Jacob tumbled off the edge of the stage to put the fire out in the snow. As he submerged his body, steam soared into the air.

Two more wolves ran at Sashmo from his front. From one knee he grabbed their heads and smashed them together, knocking them both to the ground.

"Is 'heads up' here a little too cliché?" Ellie said.

More wolves piled upon Sashmo. He struggled and managed to fight a few more off. His pain became unbearable and he was weakening by the minute. Williams let out a devious howl from the stage. He had grown tired of watching the fight from afar and he blitzed Sashmo. He took him to the ground in one swift attack. Sashmo lay motionless on the ground.

"Sashmo!" Abby screamed in fear.

Williams then returned to human form. The remaining werewolves backed away from Sashmo, leaving room for Williams to step up and deliver the final blow. Williams sauntered up to Sashmo and knelt beside him.

"It was a valiant effort for such a bumbling beast."

Williams stood, looking at Abby. "Let this be a lesson to any other creature that feels noble enough to stand in our way."

Williams turned his back to the cages. He transformed one more time into his werewolf form. His pack gathered around behind him as they approached Sashmo. They once again let out a blood curdling howl to the moon. Williams moved in slowly towards the beaten down Sashmo, who attempted to regain his footing but falls to the ground again. Williams stood upon Sashmo's back, letting out one final howl when a sudden voice from the skies interrupted.

"Oh my goodness, lots of werewolves down there," Scotty said, flying in. "What are they doing? Having a party? Doesn't look like a very fun party. There's Sashmo, he's sleeping, must be a boring party."

Led by Lilianna, a plethora of mythical creatures rushed to the scene. As Scotty and Lilianna flew in they were flanked on the ground by multiple mythical creatures. Leading the charge was the Hydra followed by various minotaurs, centaurs, hobbits, leprechauns, trolls, goblins, unicorns, and gargoyles.

"Don't let any of them get away," Lilianna called out to the herd of mythicals.

The creatures engaged in a massive battle with the werewolves, overwhelming them on pure numbers alone. After all the wolves were defeated, only Williams remained standing. The mythical creature army surrounded him as the Hydra stepped forth.

"You are a disgrace to the Council and all mythical creatures," Alpha said.

"And for your crimes, you will be judged at trial," echoed Beta.

"I don't have time for your insulant belittling Hydra. I answer to no one," Williams spoke up defiantly.

"Refusal of a trial leads to only one option," Delta said.

"I'll take my chances," Williams said.

Williams jumped in for an attack on the Hydra. The Hydra spun his body, whipping his tail around to meet him mid-jump. Williams' body sailed through the air and crashed into a nearby tree. As he hit the ground, his body fell motionless, turning back into human form.

"Agent Drozorkmog. Agent Tom. You have another to join the Hobgoblin in jail," Gamma announced.

Agent Drozorkmog and Agent Tom approached Williams and cuffed him. They lead him back to their ship. Agent Drozorkmog shot a piercing glare at Ellie before boarding and the ship taking off.

Lilianna flew to the cages and freed Abby, J.D. and Ellie. Abby rushed over to Sashmo and held him in her arms.

"Sashmo, Sashmo wake up," Abby cried, "You can't do this! Not now! Sashmo!"

She broke into tears. Ellie placed his tail around her shoulder to comfort her as a tear slipped down his scaly cheek.

"It's not fair. Sashmo. You don't deserve this."

Lilianna approached Sashmo's body. "Release him from your arms Miss Abominae," she requested.

"No, I'm not letting him go!"

"Trust me," Lilianna reassured her.

Abby let him go. She and Ellie backed away as Lilianna turned to the Hydra.

"With your blessings sirs?" Lilianna asked.

"Make it so," Epsilon said as the other heads of the Hydra nodded.

"Dark days. Darker nights," Lilianna began to hover over Sashmo. She pulled her wand out and placed it upon his forehead. "May this wand bring back what's right." Lilianna hovered away and slowly Sashmo's eyes began to flutter and open. He looked around, steadily gaining his awareness. He caught Abby's eyes.

"Sashmo!" she screamed as she flung her arms around him, kissing him.

142

"You know I thought J.D. was ugly, but after seeing a Sasquatch and Yeti kiss, he's not looking so bad," Ellie quipped. J.D. shook his head in agreement.

"I can't believe you did all this for me," Abby smiled, her tears of sorrow were replaced with tears of joy.

"Love makes you do crazy things. The Kraken was right."

"Love?"

"I've been trying to tell you for years," Sashmo hung his head in embarrassment. His cheeks blushed beneath his massive fur.

"You big dummy. There are easier ways than this." She hugged him again. Sashmo turned towards Lilianna.

"How can I ever thank you?"

"No thanks needed," Lilianna answered. "Just doing what needed to be done."

"I'll be forever grateful. If there is anything you ever need. You can count on me."

"Well look at all this. What a party it turned out to be. Sure thought it was going to be a boring party when we got here," Scotty was on a roll, "Wasn't expecting all that fighting though, really never seen that as a party game before. I'm used to something a little simpler, like Pin the Tail on the Unicorn. Maybe Elf, Elf, Gnome. Man, and somebody brought that hideous thing here," He gestured to J.D., "Talk about Debbie Downer, and where's the hors d'oeuvres? No hors d'oevures. Not even candy. I didn't sign up for this, I'm going home."

Everyone laughed at Scotty as he flew away. The Hydra approached Sashmo. "Sashmo the Sasquatch," Alpha said, his voice rang out above the laughter.

"Yes sir," Sashmo said, his nerves taking over.

"What you and your Loch Ness Monster friend have done was reckless and irresponsible," Beta scolded.

"Myself and your father created rules for a reason. To keep all of our creatures safe and to keep order intact," Delta continued.

"But," Sashmo tried to interject.

"No buts," Gamma stopped him, "For your violation of the code, you too will be judged."

Epsilon continued, "After deliberations on your actions, we, the High Council, are ready to make our ruling."

Sashmo stood up. He hugged Abby again. He thought to himself about the adventure the three of them had been on over the course of the last few weeks. No matter what the Hydra said at this moment, he was proud of what they had done. More importantly, Sashmo knew his father would be proud of him for the first time in his life.

"I accept full responsibility," Sashmo answered.

"Your father always wished that creatures, specifically you Sashmo, would be able to choose their own path," Alpha began, "Despite your actions, we believe he would be pretty proud of the path you've chosen today.

144

"Therefore, we favor pardon. In much the same way your Grandfather once pardoned our life," Beta reflected. "All creatures shall know that Sashmo the Sasquatch is a hero and savior to all mythical creatures."

Delta continued, "And that from this day forward, you shall hold the title, 'Sashmo, the Great'."

"You have made your lineage proud," Gamma concluded.

The creatures standing around erupted into a loud cheer. Sashmo turned to Abby with a huge smile on his face and gave her a giant sized hug. Ellie came over with J.D. and joined in on the hug.

"Sashmo the Great huh? That means more quests," Ellie said.

"Not now Ellie," smiled Sashmo, "Maybe later."

Epilogue: All is Well

Several weeks had passed. A beautiful beach resort sat in the middle of what appeared to be a forest. A sign read "Lost Colony Mythical Creatures Resort." Abby, Sashmo, and J.D. relaxed in lawn chairs on the beach. Suddenly Ellie came running out of the nearby resort building with a painting.

"Sashmo! You won't believe it! You know those Bob Ross tapes I've been trying to get my hands on. I don't need them anymore," Ellie continued frantically. "I just had the most vivid dream you could possibly imagine of all his shows. Look what I just did!"

Ellie turned the painting around to reveal an amazing picture of Sashmo, Abby, J.D., and himself by Loch Ness with some happy trees in the distance.

"You know this you being a hero and me being an artist thing. We should have thought about this before."

"If it had been your plan we'd never be here," joked Sashmo.

"Ellie, just relax. Look how beautiful this place is. Certainly better than the Loch," Abby responded.

"Whoa now, don't go dissing the Loch. That's going to be your home soon."

"And I just can't wait," Abby smiled, as she took Sashmo's hand.

Ellie noticed a rainbow serpent slithering along the coastline. "She might make it better," Ellie went running down the beach after the female serpent.

"You think he has a chance?" Abby asked.

"He can paint like Bob Ross now. I got you. So doesn't anyone?" Sashmo answered.

"Yeah, but you're Sashmo the Great. Of course you had a chance," Abby said with a loving smile on her face.

Sashmo leaned in to give Abby a kiss. Out of nowhere, Lilianna flew in. She seemed to be in a panic.

"Lilianna? What are doing here?" Sashmo asked. He could see she had a nervous energy about her.

"Sashmo. Abby. You have to come with me. There's trouble."

95383223R00088

Made in the USA
Lexington, KY
08 August 2018